The Science Junto

Tony Hassall

Order this book online at www.trafford.com
or email orders@trafford.com

Most Trafford titles are also available at major online book retailers.

Note for Librarians: A cataloguing record for this book is available from Library and Archives Canada at www.collectionscanada.ca/amicus/index-e.html

Printed in Victoria, BC, Canada.

ISBN: 978-1-4269-0898-9 (soft)
ISBN: 978-1-4269-0900-9 (ebook)

We at Trafford believe that it is the responsibility of us all, as both individuals and corporations, to make choices that are environmentally and socially sound. You, in turn, are supporting this responsible conduct each time you purchase a Trafford book, or make use of our publishing services. To find out how you are helping, please visit www.trafford.com/responsiblepublishing.html

Our mission is to efficiently provide the world's finest, most comprehensive book publishing service, enabling every author to experience success. To find out how to publish your book, your way, and have it available worldwide, visit us online at www.trafford.com

Trafford rev. 5/19/2009

www.trafford.com

North America & international
toll-free: 1 888 232 4444 (USA & Canada)
phone: 250 383 6864 • fax: 250 383 6804 • email: info@trafford.com

The United Kingdom & Europe
phone: +44 (0)1865 487 395 • local rate: 0845 230 9601
facsimile: +44 (0)1865 481 507 • email: info.uk@trafford.com

10 9 8 7 6 5 4 3 2 1

Table of Contents

Dedication

This book is dedicated to my beloved wife Julia, to my son Michael and his wife Leigh, to my beautiful granddaughter Paige and to Nikki who continues to inspire me.

Foreword

In this book people are generally referred to in the male gender. This is to be read in the context of 'mankind' and not taken as implying male superiority. This is done for ease of reading and women should not take offence. The majority of this work applies to women equally as it does to men. However, as a man, I have a male perspective on life and this is naturally portrayed in my writing.

Introduction

There is much that is good about science. It has released us from the religious oppression of the past, paved the way for our modern technologies and increased our life spans immensely. However there are elements of modern science that seek to lead us into darkness albeit in most cases unintentionally.

Albert Einstein said:

"The whole of science is nothing more than a refinement of everyday thinking."

This is very true and if everyday thinking consisted only of common sense, reason and a search for truth, this would not be a problem. However everyday thinking also includes pride, prejudice and dogmatic belief. If reason once prevailed in science, it is today all too often overtaken by dogma based on the loudest voices in the scientific community. Where once scientists talked of testing hypotheses, facts and experimental results, many now talk about "consensus" a word meaning agreement by majority. A majority of people once thought the Earth was the centre of the solar system, but that did not make it true. Today this consensus is being lead by the enormously popular field of environmental science.

Making matters worse, owing to the demise of religious authority scientists have now claimed the moral high ground. The prevailing view is that science is right and religion is wrong. This has elevated science to occupy a position previously held by religious leaders. Science has become the religion in power. The "bishops" of science proclaim the dogma and the mass media lap it up and spread the word like the henchmen of the inquisition.

For all time people have been herded like sheep, told how to think, what to believe and how to behave by men in authority. Political leaders, priests, witchdoctors and now scientists influence the unsophisticated and uneducated masses easily. Authority is a powerful tool. With it one can influence people to perform ritual human sacrifice, suicide bombing, or to perform mass genocide. History is littered with examples.

Authority needn't even be "legitimate" it may be self proclaimed. Merely speaking with conviction in a tone and manner that conveys an air of authority can be enough. Cult leaders are able to convince people to do insane things such as commit suicide through this technique.

In today's modern world it is often the celebrity status of the individual that confers authority. For example actors, once very low on the social rung now influence masses of humanity when their only strength is their looks and the ability to pretend they are someone they are not.

Authority kills the truth. For example in ancient Greece Aristarchus of Samos showed that the earth and the planets revolve around the sun. Yet it took eighteen hundred years before this truth was "discovered" again. This is because the truth did not suit those in authority and it was therefore suppressed. Similarly modern scientists in authority tell us that manmade carbon dioxide is causing global warming and that Darwinian evolution resulting from random chance is an undeniable fact. These two "facts" will be strongly disputed in this book.

Scientists delude themselves that they have open minds and are superior to others in exposing the truth by always applying reason over dogma, but this is an illusion. They are subject to the same prejudices and preconceived ideas as everyone else. Scientists tend to find what they already believe. If information or data comes to hand that doesn't fit with their preconceived ideas or "accepted" theory (dogma) then they reject or ignore it (or even *alter* it).

Like ninety-nine percent of the general population many scientists are unthinking dupes who are driven by the few with big egos at the top of the pile. Freethinkers in science as elsewhere are invariably cut down to size before they even get started. Throughout history major new scientific discoveries have often been made by someone who is from outside the profession or someone who at least has not been fully indoctrinated. For example Michael Faraday received virtually no formal education and Einstein was a patent clerk.

I have personally found as much bigotry, prejudice, and lying in science as I have elsewhere, perhaps more. There is a good reason for this. Many scientists do not believe in God. In other words they do not believe in a power greater than themselves. This puts them in a moral vacuum, where the truth is unimportant. The highest aspiration of these vanity driven individuals is the fulfilment of their own egos and the self satisfaction of being "right."

If you are a scientist and have begun to feel under personal attack by these words, please hear me out. These words are spoken with love of science, not contempt for it. I am a scientist myself. I love the thrill of discovery, the joy of gaining a better understanding about life's mysteries and of uncovering the truth. Scientists are mostly sincere and well meaning as are most people. Scientific method is still generally the best means we have available to determine the nature of reality. However, we are all subject to human weaknesses that we often fail to use our eyes, our ears and our ability to reason. Science must root out its own myths and dogmas and above all to admit that it has them.

If you have read this far dear reader you are probably one of very few who are willing to even consider these important matters. I am a lonely voice among just a few thinkers who are crying out in the wilderness against a massive tide of popular consensus based science. I am tired of listening to and reading the science dogma that presumes its authority and expects the world to bow down to its rhetoric. The science emperor has no clothes and I hope this book will help you to see the naked emperor as he really is and perhaps to help him back into his proper suit.

The viewpoints expressed in this book may not always lead to the absolute Truth. I am subject to the same human fallibility as everyone else. However the point is that the reader should always apply their own rigorous testing of the ideas presented against real data and apply their power of reason and experience.

This book explores the scientific world and challenges some established scientific theories via a story. It follows the journey of Bill, a modern day Freethinker from where he left off in "A Freethinkers Search for Wisdom and Truth." He continues his search here through the eyes of a scientist.

Chapter 1 - The Junto

"For having lived long, I have experienced many instances of being obliged, by better information or fuller consideration, to change opinions, even on important subjects, which I once thought right but found to be otherwise" Benjamin Franklin

"Wake up you lazy bugger!" Bill heard as he awoke from his pleasant dreams. He peered out of his sleeping bag to see Aaron grinning through the flap of the tent at him.

"How are you feeling?"

As Bill propped himself up he felt a little groggy "one too many Grand Marniers last night I reckon."

"This'll sort you out" Aaron replied as he handed Bill a steaming cup of coffee.

The sun was still below the horizon though the crows were already making their ugly squawking noise. Bill focused in on the much more tuneful magpies as he gratefully sipped his coffee and began to gather his thoughts.

They were in the outback of Queensland on a pig hunting trip. Aaron was a regular hunter for these wild animals that had become pests in the outback. He lived on the fringe of this remote region where he spent much of his time running an adventure camp for young people where they could learn outdoor skills and participate in some tough hikes and activities designed to build character.

Bill wasn't sure whether all this was building his character, but he enjoyed Aaron's company and it was a good break from his normal life. Aaron was a fit man in his fifties who had done many things in his life, including for some time being a Methodist Minister. Despite his rough exterior he had a gentle and kindly nature and the depth of his wisdom never ceased to amaze Bill.

They had taken a good haul of pigs the day before with the motor bikes and dogs which were safely in the chiller unit that Aaron towed behind his four wheel drive Ute. "I reckon we've got enough pigs to take home" Aaron declared. "Today we'll do a peaceful hunt on foot. We'll just take old Sam with us. He's pretty quiet and won't go nuts at the scent of a pig. He won't let us down either, if there's a pig around you can be sure old Sam will tell us where it is." Bill knew that Aaron was speaking affectionately about his favourite dog that had been mostly by his side for ten years.

Bill felt a keen sense of adventure as they kitted up with rifles, knives, water and a few rations for the morning hunt. They walked in silence through the scrub which was fairly sparse but offered them reasonable cover in places and was according to Aaron good pig country. Suddenly Aaron stopped, put his finger to his lips and whispered "this rooting looks pretty fresh" as he pointed to the ground where the sods had been freshly turned over by foraging pigs, "they're really close."

Bill's heart started to pound heavily in his chest as he felt the thrill and anticipation of the hunt that so many men must have felt over tens of thousands of years of their history. He quietly slid a round into the chamber of his rifle and set the bolt to the half cock position.

Aaron bent down to touch some droppings. "Still warm" he murmured. Just then Sam started to run around madly with his nose to the ground, his tail high in the air and in a flash tore off into the thick undergrowth howling and barking for all he was worth. "I'd hate to think what the *non-quiet* dogs would be like" Bill chuckled to Aaron who just grinned back and hurried off, following the howling dog into the scrub.

For a while the dog's howling became fainter and then the noise changed altogether. There was a loud squealing from a distressed pig and the dog noises alternated between excited howling and growling to a pathetic wailing.

"Damn!" Aaron yelled, breaking into a run as they approached the ruckus. They finally broke through the bush and came upon the scene where the dog had bailed up a huge Boar against some rocks. Bill had never seen a pig that size. His heart fell as he saw what was happening. The Boar had got the better of the dog and was mauling it with its tusks. Aaron screamed as he leapt into the fray, the large knife in his hand slid deeply into the heart of the squealing pig.

When the pig had finally stopped moving Aaron picked himself up and turned his attention to Sam who was in a bad way. "Ah you poor old thing" he sighed as he stroked the head of his old pal. He's a gonna I'm afraid. I guess he was just getting a bit old and slow. Would you do me a favour Bill?"

Bill knew what Aaron meant; he could see there was no hope for the old dog. "Sure Aaron, no problem." Aaron slowly walked away as Bill closed the bolt and pulled the trigger.

In silence they made a hollow in the ground with their knives and sticks, and covered the body of the dog with rocks as best they could. Aaron quickly cut the legs and rump from the Boar which they shared into their carry packs made for the purpose.

When they had finally finished Aaron looked at Bill with an uncharacteristic sad expression, his eyes glistening with held back tears. "If you don't mind Bill I'd like to walk back to the camp on my own. You know the way back. I want to take a slightly longer route."

"No problem Aaron."

As Bill walked back to the camp he became engrossed in his thoughts. Being alone with nature was an opportunity to reflect and to think about where he was going with his life. He had written his first book and was pleased with the result, but it hadn't been a commercial success and he needed to earn a living.

He had not long since completed a Master of Science degree in Agriculture and thought this might provide some opportunities. He had come to love science, despite having spent much of his working life as an accountant. I could go back to university and try to complete a PhD if I could get some funding, he thought. I don't need a big income now with Charlie grown up and Sarah working. The more he thought about it the more he started to like the idea.

The walk back to the camp seemed to go quickly despite the heavy load of meat he had on his back. He unloaded his share of the pig into the chiller and started to pack up the camp ready for the trip home. As he was putting his gear into the vehicle he heard a shout. "Bill, help me!"

He turned and saw Aaron hobbling towards him, his leg completely bound up in his shirt which he had ripped up. He no longer carried his pack and was using his rifle as a kind of walking stick. Aaron looked unnaturally pale as Bill ran towards him, grabbed his arm and threw it over his shoulder.

"Bloody snake!" Aaron grumbled as Bill helped him shuffle back to the camp.

"Did you see what kind it was?" asked Bill anxiously, knowing, if it was a bad one their only hope was to get him to a hospital really quickly.

"Yeah, taipan" Aaron replied. "You'd better get that satellite phone out of the Ute."

Bill's worst fears were realised. The taipan was one of the deadliest snakes in the world. He rushed to the vehicle, turned on the satellite phone and dialled 000. It seemed to take a frustratingly long time to communicate the details of where they were to the emergency services. "Thank goodness for GPS" Bill said as he hung up and turned his attention back to Aaron, "they're sending an ambulance chopper."

Bill knew that time was now the critical factor and Aaron needed to keep as still as possible but stay upright so as to delay the movement of the venom to his heart. Aaron had done the right thing in binding up his leg to slow down the circulation. As they waited Bill kept saying encouraging words to Aaron, but secretly he became very concerned as Aaron began to slip in and out of consciousness.

After what seemed an eternity Bill heard the welcome throbbing noise of the helicopter as it came into view. The rush of air he felt as it came in to land was like the breath of God and as it came to rest two paramedics leapt out with a stretcher. Bill was very grateful as they took charge of the situation. Aaron was now completely unconscious.

"Do you know what kind the snake was?"

"Yeah he reckoned it was a taipan" Bill replied.

"OK" replied the officer, his expression not giving anything away. "Sorry, you can't come with us. We'll be going to the

Toowoomba Base Hospital if you'd like to catch up with us there."

The helicopter was in the air again minutes after landing. Bill quickly packed up the remains of the camp and wasted no time driving back to Aaron's place. After tending to the dogs he told a neighbour about the situation before speeding off in his car towards Toowoomba.

When he arrived at the hospital he anxiously enquired about Aaron. They informed him that Aaron was still unconscious in a critical condition and he had been given a second dose of anti-venom. "You can stay in our waiting room if you like. We'll let you know if there's any change" said the nurse sympathetically.

Bill paced up and down the waiting room, his mind racing. He hadn't noticed anyone enter the room, but a voice disturbed him from his thoughts.

"Don't worry, Aaron will be OK" said the kindly voice. Bill looked up, startled and saw the elderly gentleman he knew as Hamish standing there smiling at him.

"How did you know we were here?" Bill asked. He was very surprised to see Hamish whom he had met only once before in similarly extraordinary circumstances when his life was at something of a crossroad. He knew that Aaron belonged to some kind of group in which Hamish appeared to be the leader.

"It was no problem" Hamish replied cryptically. "As I said Aaron will be OK. Let's talk about you. You've been thinking about your future?" Although this was posed as a question it was as if Hamish already knew the answer.

"Yeah, I have been thinking about my future" Bill replied, not bothering to ask how he knew, realising that he wouldn't get a satisfactory answer from this mysterious man.

"And have you decided?"

"Well I was thinking of going back to Uni to do a PhD. I enjoyed doing my Masters and it might open up a new career path. I'm not getting any younger though."

"Age is never a problem" Hamish chuckled. "It's only attitude to your age that matters. Doing something you really have a passion for sounds like a good idea. Perhaps if you do decide to go that way, there might be something you can do for me."

"Oh, what's that?" asked Bill, intrigued.

Hamish did not answer the question directly, but invited Bill to a dinner meeting the following week in Brisbane to discuss the matter.

Just then the nurse came in and said "your friend is going to be fine, he's recovering nicely. You can go and see him now."

Hamish shook Bill's hand and said he would catch up with Aaron soon, allowing Bill to visit Aaron alone.

"Thank God you're OK" he said as he saw Aaron's smiling face now propped up in bed. "I've just been talking to Hamish in the waiting room."

"The old codger didn't even bother to come in and see me" Aaron replied showing annoyance, but in a jocular way.

"He said he'd catch up with you soon. He seemed to know you were going to be OK" Bill said.

"Yeah that wouldn't surprise me. Nothing surprises me with Hamish. How did you get on packing up the camp?"

"All's well, your neighbours are going to look after your dogs."

"Thanks Bill, and thanks for getting me to hospital. They reckon I couldn't have lasted much longer without that anti-venom."

"No problem, I'm just glad you're OK" Bill replied.

They chatted for a time before Bill said he'd better get home. He hadn't even rung Sarah to let her know where he was.

Bill told Sarah, his wife of twenty-five years, about his adventures and about his plans to continue his studies. She was as always very supportive.

As arranged Bill went to the meeting in Brisbane the following week. He was greeted by a grinning and fully recovered Aaron at the door. A large dinner table was set with Hamish sitting at the head and most of the other places already occupied.

On seeing Bill enter the room Hamish got up, shook his hand warmly and introduced him to the people around the table, offering first names only and without elaborating on who they were. There were a diverse range of men and women.

The last places at the table were filled and when they were all seated Hamish called on one of the group to say grace and the dinner began. Conversation during the dinner was little more than social chit chat, no discussion that would give Bill any clue as to what the group was about.

After dinner Hamish called the meeting to order, at which the others fell silent and Hamish began.

"We are pleased to welcome Bill to our gathering this evening. You are all familiar with the work Bill was doing on the email group he set up to debate the Big questions of life." There was a murmuring of acknowledgement. "Aaron was a member of that group and has come to know him quite well" Hamish continued.

He then turned to look directly at Bill and explained that this group of twelve people met periodically to discuss important matters concerning mankind. "We all share a strong desire to uphold the Truth and to uplift ourselves along with our fellow man. We take turns at preparing and presenting a discussion on a topic that may be concerning us. Issues may include morality, politics, religion, industry, crime, education, actually all manner of things about the world and the direction in which its people are headed.

After the group has discussed the issue, we resolve whether there is something we ought to do about it. If action is to be taken, members who are best suited to the task are charged with the responsibility of carrying it out. Actions may involve publications, communication with certain people or sometimes direct engagement. However the actions we take are not done in the name of this group, they are carried out by each member in their normal walk of life. It is very important that the existence of this group remain secret. Do you understand the reason for this?"

"Yes" replied Bill, "I think so. Secret societies arouse suspicion about their motives and they become a target for groups who wish to undermine their activities or they are sometimes made a scapegoat."

"Quite so" Hamish nodded. "Also by remaining hidden we are able to have complete control over our membership."

"It sounds a lot like the Junto that Benjamin Franklin set up!" Bill exclaimed.

"Yes, you are right Bill. We are in fact a Junto, except that Benjamin Franklin was not the founder of this particular one. Today there are many groups that call themselves a Junto, some of which have used the Franklin model. The word itself is of course merely the Latin word for meeting. Most of these groups however have no direct connection with Franklin or with us for that matter. Our particular Junto has associations that go back quite a long way, though I am not at liberty to go into that right now."

Bill had noticed that there were actually only eleven people seated at the table apart from himself. Hamish, as if reading his thoughts, now turned back towards the others in the attentive audience. "Aaron believes that Bill would make an admirable member to fill our vacant seat. From what I have seen of Bill, I am inclined to agree with him." Several of the others nodded.

Hamish then turned back to Bill and asked "how would you like to join our Junto?"

Bill had no hesitation in saying "I'd love to." His experiences with both Aaron and Hamish had taught him that this was a very wise and worthy group, and he felt very privileged to be asked.

"Very well, I will have to ask you to leave the room briefly please, to put a motion to the group." Aaron escorted Bill into an adjacent room and left him alone with his thoughts. After several minutes Aaron returned grinning, nodding and beckoning him back into the dining room. As he entered there was an eruption of applause along with calls of congratulations and welcome to the Junto.

Hamish raised his hand to cut off the applause and said "before we can admit you we require you to make certain commitments to us." With that he handed Bill a sheet of paper and waited while he read through it and nodded his agreement.

Hamish then stood and began.

"Please stand and hold your right hand over your heart while answering these questions:

Do you believe in God?"

"Yes."

"Do you believe there is a universal system that rewards virtue and punishes sin either in this life or hereafter?"

"Yes."

"Do you sincerely declare that you love mankind in general, no matter what profession or religion?"

"I do."

"Do you believe any person ought to be harmed in body, name or property, for their speculative opinions, or their external way of worship?"

"No."

"Do you love truth, and will you endeavour impartially to find and receive it yourself and to communicate it always to this Junto?"

"Yes."

"Will you promise to respect all members of this Junto, their opinions and their right to express them?"

"Yes."

"Do you swear under God that these answers you have given are true and sincere?"

"Yes."

"Welcome to the Junto!"

There was another big round of applause and Bill felt a wave of pride wash over him.

After the ceremony Hamish and Aaron took Bill back into the adjacent room while the others took their coffee. "Bill the other day I mentioned that there was something you could do for us" Hamish said quietly.

"Sure" Bill replied, somewhat apprehensively.

"Well, we are concerned with the way some elements of the scientific community have been heading lately. You are about to embark on a scientific career and this could fit in nicely with our agenda in this area."

"OK, you'd like me to get a message out there or gather some information?"

"Well there's a bit more to it than that" Hamish responded. "This is a far reaching issue. We would like to see a new Junto formed just for the purpose of monitoring the situation and if possible to enlighten and even change the direction of scientific thought and action."

"And you want me to set up this Junto?"

"Yes. You will have Aaron to help you. He will be a member of your "Science Junto" but you and he will be the only ones permitted to know about the existence of our original Junto. You may say that you and some friends are setting up a group to discuss scientific matters or something of that nature.

You will choose your members very carefully, so you will need to get to know them quite well before you ask them. They need to be sincere people with quite open minds and a willingness to work for Truth and for the betterment of mankind. They need to be people you feel confident will accept our entry criteria because you will ask them to adopt a similar creed. The members will be recruited from various branches of science to provide a diverse range of input. Aaron will help you to decide. Are you willing to carry out this task?"

"Sounds like fun!" Bill responded enthusiastically. "What are your main concerns with science?"

Hamish thought for a long moment before replying "we are concerned about the morality of science, its atheistic position and the way that it now influences our political leaders into making poor and unbalanced decisions. Science is also being used as a tool to carry out the agendas of an evil element that seeks to undermine the progress of mankind along with his noble mission. We are particularly concerned about the misguidance of our young people who are of course our future."

"OK I'm in, sounds like a serious and worthy mission!" Bill exclaimed.

Chapter 2 - Genetics

"Reason must be our last judge and guide in everything" John Locke

Bill returned from the Junto meeting feeling inspired and with a strong sense of purpose. It was no problem enrolling in a PhD with his strong academic record and he was able to obtain funding through one of the government-industry partnership bodies that funded research into agriculture.

The only problem was that he would have to spend most of his time at the university to be close to resources. This meant he would be away most of the week and only able to return home for the weekends. Sarah was apprehensive about this at first, but said she would cope and was happy that Bill was doing something that he really wanted to do. She was busy and very much involved with her job in education in any case.

The topic he had chosen for his PhD was to do with genetic modification of crops. GM had become a hot topic since the technology had been developed to manipulate genes. He was interested partly in the science of GM but also in the economics and the social ramifications of it. With his background in finance he was well qualified to analyse the costs and benefits of GM and this was to form a substantial part of his thesis.

He thought the best place to live was on campus in a university hostel. This way he wouldn't have to worry about meals and would be able to devote most of his time to study and to his recruiting task. He was a little anxious about this as he had spent time in one of these institutions in his youth. Bill was now middle aged and the frivolity, partying and noise of young students would not be to his liking.

He explained his anxiety to the lady in charge of hostel accommodation and she was able to allay his fears. "Don't worry about that" she said, "we have a hostel that caters mostly for international students. Most of them are full fee paying and are under great pressure from their families back home to achieve results. You won't see any partying there. We have a few other mature aged students like you in there as well. I'm sure you'll enjoy it."

Bill's spirits were lifted temporarily, but were dashed again when he entered his room in the hostel. "Positively claustrophobic" he muttered to himself as he surveyed the tiny room, "I wonder if prison cells are worse than this." A desk, some book shelves, a bed that was too short for him and an old wooden chair that reminded him of a Van Gogh painting. It was all a far cry from the open spaces he was used to.

"Well I've made my decision" he thought, "better make the best of it. Must keep telling myself I'm on a mission and not be negative" he lectured himself. With that thought he went to explore the building looking for bathrooms and other facilities. He passed several students in the hallway, none of whom made eye contact with him, though one did at least acknowledge him and smiled as he tried to make a friendly greeting.

He eventually stumbled on a common room with an old television set in it where there sat a man with a straggly beard, dressed in jeans and a rather scruffy old tee shirt and probably in his thirties. "Gidday, my name's Bill" he said.

"Jeff" the man replied as he stood up and shook Bill's hand warmly. "It's good to see a friendly face. Not that I'm racist or anything, but these Asians aren't very sociable. I've been here twelve months and they hardly say a word."

"I guess they're a bit shy being so far away from home, struggling with the culture, our language and so on" Bill suggested.

"Yeah I guess so, but they have no trouble socialising with each other" Jeff replied sceptically. "Anyway what are you in for?" he said gesturing to the barred windows.

Bill grinned "yeah it does feel a bit like a prison" and went on to explain a little about his proposed project on GM.

"That sounds interesting" Jeff responded, "I'm also doing a PhD, but for me its environmental science."

"That's pretty popular these days" Bill remarked.

"Yeah, there's a lot of bullshit in it though. I'm getting a bit disillusioned with it. It's a bit like a religion for some of these people I have to work with. But enough of that, I'm getting hungry, do you know where the dining hall is?"

Jeff escorted Bill to the large dining room from where there emanated a noisy throng with the clatter of knives and forks and the chatter of about a hundred people eating, mostly young people of Asian appearance. Bill smiled back at the friendly ladies who served him generous portions of an appetising looking meal.

"Wow this looks pretty good" he said to Jeff who had been joking and flirting with one of the ladies behind the servery.

"Yeah they make some good grub" Jeff chuckled. "We're lucky; they reckon our hostel has the best cook on account of us being the best behaved. It's some consolation."

Jeff led Bill to a table where several other mature aged students were sitting. "Welcome to the geriatrics table" one said as Bill introduced himself. It was a diverse group and Bill enjoyed chatting with them over dinner about their backgrounds and fields of study.

After dinner Bill retired to his room to reflect on his mission. He knew that it would be tough finding the right kind of people from the science community for his Junto. Mature people would usually be set in their ways of thinking and would not be useful unless they were already like-minded people. Even if they were rare freethinkers, they were likely to have become entrenched in their careers and the "system" and would not risk losing their position to further the Truth.

Younger people on the other hand were more likely to be open minded, more likely to take risks and university was certainly a good place to find them. Perhaps people that were the "rebel" type would be best as they were more open to new ideas, but he didn't want any maniacs. People that were too religious would not do as they would be too fixed in their beliefs; on the other hand he didn't want atheists either because atheism was one of Hamish's concerns.

Then there was the great bulk of humanity that basically doesn't give a damn. He suspected that the right people were probably out there but how was he going to find them? He went to sleep thinking on it and as he awoke he had an idea.

He would call overtly for scientifically minded people to join a group to discuss scientific matters and from this group he would secretly select individuals for his Junto once he got to know them and could assess their suitability. He constructed a notice that read as follows:

Wanted

Open-minded scientists to debunk science and religion

Must not be politically correct

Must be serious about finding the meaning of life

Meeting in the park Tuesdays 1pm - 2pm

He thought that the playful nature of this invitation might attract some interesting candidates. Anyway it would be fun and he had nothing to lose. He discretely placed his advertisement on several notice boards on his way to the agricultural science faculty building.

Bill was excited though apprehensive as he climbed the stairs of the faculty building to meet his PhD supervisor for the first time. Tim was younger than he expected, probably in his early thirties and was very warm and friendly as he greeted Bill. "Come and sit down and we'll discuss this project of yours."

Tim explained his own background to Bill, that he had himself not long since completed a PhD thesis on plant genetics. He was a junior lecturer in the Department and worked under the supervision of Professor Bob Natal. "I'll introduce you to the Professor later" Tim said, "he will also be one of your supervisors. He's very well respected in the genetics field so that should not be a problem for you. Basically I'll be your day to day supervisor and Bob will just help to sign off your key milestones.

I'm looking forward to working with you on this project. I think it's really worthwhile; there's huge scope for GM in agriculture to increase food production immensely. We are working on more drought tolerant strains of grain and herbicide resistant crops that should help not only our Australian farmers but have great potential in some of the third world countries."

Tim's enthusiasm was infectious; he positively glowed as he explained the potential for GM crops to solve world hunger and famine. He explained that he had spent a year in an African country doing voluntary service after leaving school and had been profoundly affected by the experience. He previously had idealistic notions wherein he blamed the West for allowing people to starve in Africa. It was his feelings of guilt that inspired him to volunteer for service in the first place. But while he was there he was apparently influenced by an African woman, a community leader who convinced him that problems with hunger in Africa were internally caused. She explained that it was largely corrupt politics, poor education and lack of good production systems. She persuaded him that food aid did nothing in the long term other than create more dependency. "How would you like to be fed like some animal in the zoo?" she had said to him angrily.

Bill listened attentively while Tim went on to explain the background of his research and the work he was collaborating on with others. Finally Bill was able to explain his own ideas for research. "I have a strong interest in the potential for GM strains to achieve better disease resistance that will reduce the need for chemicals" he explained.

"Sure," Tim replied "it's an area we haven't done much work on, but the potential is again enormous. It's a wonder those organic people haven't jumped at the chance to reduce chemical usage."

"You'd think so wouldn't you," Bill agreed "but the organic movement is anti GM from what I understand. I hear a lot in the press about the risks of GM, what's your take on that?"

"Oh that's all just paranoia" Tim scoffed. "The biggest problem is that people think we're a bunch of Frankensteins creating hybrid creatures they've seen in horror movies. But that's rubbish; the average Joe just doesn't understand the science. The public don't realise that we've been doing genetic modification ever since agriculture began, but its all been haphazard and subject to trial and error. Now we're able to reduce the trial and error and get results much more quickly with modern gene technology. Like all food products they'll go through rigorous testing to assess any potential risks anyway."

"I probably need to update my knowledge about the science of GM myself?" Bill said hesitantly, "I'm a bit rusty."

"I'll be glad to give you a tutorial Bill, just as soon as we've had a cuppa."

Just then a short chubby man with a dark complexion stepped into the room and said "so this is our new student, he's a bit on the mature side!"

Tim appeared flustered as he introduced the man as Professor Bob Natal.

"It's a privilege to meet you at last Professor" Bill said genuinely. "You're very famous. It seems like I've seen your name on hundreds of scientific papers."

"Yes I suppose I have put out a few" the Professor replied rather immodestly. "Sorry I can't stay and chat – busy, busy" and with that he left.

"Sorry about that" Tim said apologetically when the Professor was out of earshot. "He doesn't have much tact."

"That's OK" Bill replied. "I guess he must be busy."

"Hmmm" Tim muttered.

Tim then escorted Bill to the staff canteen. As they made their coffee he was introduced to several other staff and postgraduate students, most of whom warmly welcomed him to the faculty. After they had sat down a rather dishevelled looking woman of about forty came over and said to Tim "have you spliced any fish genes onto a peanut today?"

"This is Hillary" Tim said. "She's one of these organic nutters that wants to drag us all back into the dark ages. She does Morris Dancing in her spare time."

"Oh, pleased to meet you" Bill said politely, ignoring the banter. "I've done some work on organics myself."

Hillary smiled "come and see me sometime, I might have some tutorial work for you."

They chatted over coffee about genetics and this lead to the subject of Darwinian evolution. Bill was slightly annoyed with the way both Tim and Hillary talked about it as if it was an undisputed fact. He couldn't help saying he didn't believe in Darwinism. What a reaction this caused.

"So you're a bloody fundamentalist!" Hillary snapped. "I suppose you're going to tell us that your God made the world six thousand years ago and that dinosaurs never existed."

"Err no" Bill replied defensively. "I'm certainly not a fundamentalist and I didn't say I don't believe in evolution. I just don't believe in Darwinism."

"What do you mean by that?" Tim asked.

"I mean I don't think it all just happened by random chance. That's what Darwinism forces you to accept. It's like believing you can create the Taj Mahal by throwing sand into the wind."

"Well maybe if you threw enough sand in the air" Hillary suggested.

"Perhaps for a little experiment you could go out and start chucking sand in the air and see how far you get" Tim chirped, grinning back at Bill. "You'll have to excuse us Bill, I'm afraid we did have a guy in the faculty until recently who was a fundamentalist. He did believe that everything in the Bible was true, even the stuff that contradicts itself. I guess you're a bit of a novelty not being a Darwinist but not being a fundamentalist either. You're quite right, Darwinian evolution is certainly only a theory, and we shouldn't talk about it as if it was a fact."

Hillary remained aloof however and Bill heard her muttering something about "misogynist right wing Bible bashers" as she went out.

"Don't worry about Hillary" Tim said as soon as she had left. "She's full of it. She used to have some ideals about agricultural production, but nowadays she's become bitter and twisted and lives in an ivory tower."

"That's OK" Bill replied "we all have our crosses to bear."

After the coffee break they returned to Tim's office where he proceeded to give Bill a refresher course in genetics. He drew a rough diagram on the whiteboard of the double helix spiral ladder shape of the DNA molecule that is the coding system of life. "It's really very simple Bill. A gene, which is either a complete DNA molecule or a part of one, is very similar to the binary system we use to code computers. Each rung of the ladder consists of a pair of bases. There are only four bases involved and they are commonly referred to by their initials A, T, C and G. A can pair only pair with T and C can only pair with G. So each rung of the ladder can be an A-T, a T-A, a C-G or a G-C. The coding system we call genetics is merely the order that these rungs appear on the DNA molecule. Whether you're a dog, a cat or a water melon the chemistry is just the same. It's only the complexity that changes."

Bill listened attentively "the way you explain it, it's as simple as ABC. So the genetic code contains the *information* for how to build the organism. How does the information get there though? The binary code we use for computers is just a row of numbers on its own, but it's the way we use this code to create software that's important. What are the laws of chemistry or physics that determines the sequence of a particular DNA strand?"

"I see what you're driving at" Tim looked slightly perplexed. "Of course we derive from Darwin's theory that it was all a result of chance mutations and the best adapted creature survived. I guess we all just accept that explanation these days without giving it much thought."

"So, did we get to the rational human being that's capable of flying spaceships to Mars from an amoeba by a series of chance mutations?" Bill asked cheekily.

"Apparently yes, though it sounds pretty unlikely when you really think about it. Our DNA is only about two percent different from a chimpanzee you know" Tim continued defensively.

"Isn't that a problem for Darwinists though?" Bill asked.

"How do you mean?"

"I'm talking about the huge divide between animals and humans. You can plot the evolutionary curve over millions of years up to the ape satisfactorily, but when you look at the grunting oaf that is the ape and compare it with the creation and achievement of mankind, there's no comparison."

"There are a few grunting oafs down the hall in this department" Tim grinned.

"I'll see if I can bring in a chimp one day to have tea with them. They might get on pretty well" Bill chuckled. "But seriously we humans have about twenty-five thousand genes right?"

Tim nodded.

"Well if we're ninety-eight percent chimp that only leaves a few hundred genes to account for all the differences between animals and humans as well as the multitude of non-environmental differences between individual humans."

"Yeah it is a bit of a mystery."

"Also I read recently about some research that shows chimps have actually undergone more so-called positively selected gene changes through the process of natural selection than humans have."

There followed an uncomfortably long silence before Tim finally said "OK Socrates aren't we supposed to be talking about GM crops?"

"Err yeah, sorry Tim, tell me about GM crops."

"Well you understand the process of genetic engineering and that DNA chemistry is the same for all living things. The fact is that we've been genetically modifying our crops ever since agriculture began. None of our food crops are "natural" varieties. They've been genetically modified through our breeding programs. If we had to rely on the natural varieties of grain for example we'd all be starving. Genetic engineering is just a tool to improve our cropping systems still further."

"So you're saying that it's really no different to what we've always done in agriculture, just a more efficient way of doing it?" Bill enquired.

"Precisely," Tim replied "and we haven't just been doing it with crops, but with our animals as well. We've been genetically selecting cows for better milk, sheep for better wool, dogs to help guide blind people and so on."

"So it's not Frankenstein stuff then?"

"Of course not!" Tim exclaimed. "Remember we aren't creating any new species here. GM wheat is still wheat."

The discussion then moved to aspects of GM that directly impacted Bill's area of research. Tim then gave Bill some advice about planning his research and they arranged to meet weekly from there on to discuss progress.

Bill spent the next few days finding his way around the university and its systems as well as meeting some of the other postgraduate students. He got the impression that Professor Natal was not very well liked by those in his Department. His international reputation seemed to have been gained at the expense of his students and the staff that reported to him. By all accounts he was not good at giving credit where it was due and ensured that he was the one to present new findings to conferences and so on. He was also very snobbish which suited Bill because it meant he didn't have much to do with him.

Bill's nights were mostly spent studying, but occasionally he got together with Jeff over a bottle of wine and they quickly struck up a friendship. It turned out that Jeff was something of a seeker like Bill. He had been brought up in a devout Christian family but like many young people had become disillusioned. In recent years he had been dabbling with Buddhism which he had come across through his connections with the environmental movement. However lately he was also becoming disillusioned with that. He seemed quite confused in his thoughts and had real problems reconciling his religious faith with what he learned in science. Bill invited him to his first meeting in the park.

The signs had created some interest and several people comprised the first gathering. Bill explained that the group was to be a forum to discuss topical scientific issues with a sceptical and open mind and to seek the Truth regardless of political correctness. The group decided to call itself the *science sceptics* and it was agreed that each week one person in turn would deliver a talk on a topical scientific issue and this would be followed by a discussion session among the group. Jeff volunteered to present the first speech.

Chapter 3 - Environmentalism

"Such is the respect paid to science that the most absurd opinions may become current, provided they are expressed in language, the sound of which recalls some well-known scientific phrase" James Clerk Maxwell

To a small group of attentive students Jeff delivered his speech entitled "Climate Change" as follows:

""‘*Everyone complains about the weather but no one does anything about it.*" That was the dry wit of Mark Twain. It was amusing because everyone knew that we can't do anything about the weather. But these days we think we can change the weather. In fact some people think we can change the weather *catastrophically*."

Jeff looked around his audience to gauge the interest from his opening as he disclosed the first page of a large flip chart he had brought along. It contained two quotes:

- *"The entire global scientific community has a consensus on the question that human beings are responsible for global warming"*
  Al Gore in an interview at the Cannes Film festival May 2006
- *"Climate change will claim hundreds of thousands of lives"*
  Stephen Tindale Executive director of Greenpeace -the Guardian 3 March 2006

Jeff allowed time for his audience to read them before flipping to the next chart as he continued, "but hang on a minute, we've heard this sort of thing before!"

The second chart contained two further quotes:

- *"The rapid cooling of the earth since world war two is in accord with the increased air pollution associated with industrialisation and an exploding population"*
  Reid Bryson, Environmental Roulette 1971
- *"The threat of a new ice age must now stand alongside nuclear war as a likely source of wholesale death and misery for mankind"*
  Nigel Calder, International Wildlife June 1975

"So" Jeff continued, "in only thirty years our climate alarmists have gone from manmade catastrophic global cooling to manmade catastrophic global warming. They were wrong then and they are wrong now. I'm going to show you that global warming is nothing more than a load of hot air! By the way have you noticed that it's not politically correct to say *global warming* any more? Now its *climate change.* So the alarmists can point to any drought, any cyclone or any flood and say it's caused by manmade climate change. Fill in the blank they can't lose with that kind of logic.

First let's consider whether the planet is really warming" Jeff stated, as he presented a graph showing that global temperatures had indeed increased over the latter part of the twentieth century, but the trend had tailed off and there had been no net increase over the last ten years since 1998.

"But this is only a graph of the last hundred years or so since we've actually been recording the temperature. If we look further back we see a different picture." He then showed a one thousand year graph compiled by a Harvard University team which published results in 2003 of a comprehensive study of world temperatures. This showed other warming and cooling periods with world temperatures in the Middle Ages higher than today's. This graph also showed that a little Ice Age set in about 1300, during which the world cooled dramatically followed by a warming period since 1900. "So when we say that the Earth is warmer we need to say compared to when? Compared to 1960 we are warmer but not compared to the medieval warm period.

If temperatures have been increasing, is human produced CO_2 the culprit as claimed by Al Gore and his cronies? First of all I don't dispute that CO_2 has been increasing, but let's not forget what a minute portion CO_2 is of the earth's atmosphere. It's about zero point zero three percent. That's three molecules of CO_2 per ten thousand molecules of atmosphere. I can't even show that on a pie chart, it wouldn't even register. Even if the amount of CO_2 in the atmosphere doubled it would still be a tiny fraction. You have to ask yourself if this tiny fraction could be the cause of global warming."

Jeff pointed again to the hundred year graph "now see how the temperature *drops* from 1940 to 1975. That's why the alarmists were working themselves into a frenzy about manmade global *cooling* back in the seventies. Our emissions were rising rapidly between 1940 and 1975, so if the CO_2 theory was correct, we would expect to see temperature increase, not decrease over that period. Look also at what's happened since 1998, the increasing temperature trend that started in the 1970s has stopped! And yet emissions have continued to go up more than ever. Why isn't the temperature still rising in line with emissions? The CO_2 theory is obviously wrong!

You will have seen Al Gore in his movie strutting along a long graph that purports to show that there is a long term correlation between atmospheric CO_2 levels and temperatures. In this he is correct, but he has it backwards. Global temperature increase causes more atmospheric CO_2, not the other way around. This is because most of our CO_2 is dissolved in the sea. As temperatures rise, so the sea gives up more of the CO_2.

Now if I haven't yet convinced you that the CO_2 climate change theory is incorrect, let me show you something even more interesting. The greenhouse gas theory says that CO_2 in the upper atmosphere forms a barrier that is supposed to stop heat from radiating back out. If you have ever been up near your ceiling on a hot day you'll know what I'm talking about. The heat gets trapped in by the ceiling and it's hotter near the ceiling than near the floor.

So, if that was really happening, we should find that the temperatures are heating up the upper atmosphere, below where the CO_2 barrier is supposed to be. But this is not the case!" Jeff exclaimed as he presented some data taken both from weather balloons and satellites showing that temperatures in the upper atmosphere had not increased in line with surface temperatures. "That blows away the whole greenhouse gas theory!" Jeff threw his hands up emphatically.

"So, if it's not manmade greenhouse gases that have caused temperature rises, what else could it be?" Jeff displayed another graph that correlated sun spot cycles with global temperatures. "It's a pretty good match! Look, I can't be sure that sun spot cycles are the cause of the warming, but it's surely more likely than manmade greenhouse gases. Don't forget the earth has had many ice ages in the past. In the last ice age only fifteen thousand years ago glaciers and ice a mile thick covered most of the USA and half of Europe. That's real climate change for you! No one really knows for sure what causes ice ages, but one thing we do know is that they're not caused by man's activities."

Jeff paused momentarily for his message to sink in before continuing. "I wonder how many times I've heard on the news that scientists are agreed, there is a *consensus* that climate change is caused by manmade CO_2. "The debate is over" we often hear climate scientists saying. Well I say to you that the debate hasn't even *begun* and there is no consensus among scientists. In fact the whole concept of consensus is foreign to science. Science deals in facts and the weight of evidence and rational argument based on these things. The only thing we know for sure about the extra CO_2 in the atmosphere is that our plants will grow better. CO_2 is plant food, it is not a poison and it is not pollution.

I have here a copy of an open letter dated December 2007 to the Secretary-General of the United Nations signed by one hundred expert scientists from around the world stating that climate change is a natural phenomenon and it is not possible to stop it. The letter further states that "attempts to prevent global climate change from occurring are ultimately futile, and constitute a tragic misallocation of resources." This letter and the scientists who wrote it have been ignored by all main stream media.

Now I would like to talk more specifically about our climate in Australia. We often hear media reports that the recent drought in Australia has been caused by the same CO_2 induced climate change. But has the temperature increase caused the drought?" Jeff then showed a hundred year rainfall map for Australia and one for average temperatures. "As you can see our current rainfall is nothing unusual and the trend in rainfall bares absolutely no resemblance to the temperature map. So once again the climate alarmists have it utterly and completely wrong. There is no science or statistical evidence anywhere that links global warming with less rainfall. Science actually tells us that the opposite is true. Warmer temperatures cause higher evaporation which in turn causes more humidity and consequently more rainfall. We know this is true because regions near the equator are among the wettest areas on earth.

In relation to Australia I'd also like to talk about cyclones. Al Gore and company have been telling us that cyclones are increasing in intensity due to manmade global warming. But again this is completely false. The strongest cyclone, with the lowest pressure of nine hundred and twenty-one hectopascals, ever recorded on the Australian mainland happened at Onslow in 1961. The second strongest was cyclone Amy in January 1980 that flattened the town of Goldsworthy. You might also ask are we getting more cyclones now. Again, no! The highest number of recorded cyclones we've had in one year was in 1963 when we had sixteen."

Jeff again paused to gauge the interest from his audience. "So if what I've told you is true, why all the fuss about global warming and mass hysteria? First and foremost I blame the media. What really sells newspapers is negative sensationalism. You've seen the headlines: "Increasing drought, lost vital ecosystems, rising sea levels, massive floods, spread of disease and malnutrition, species extinctions." The big cuddly looking polar bear is pictured on a small ice sheet. The polar bear has survived much greater climate changes in the past than the current one but of course this little bit of information is never offered. The worst thing about the media is that it plays on our fears. They keep thrusting these shocking and disastrous scenarios in our faces. The constant negative imagery hooks our emotions so much that we can no longer think rationally.

Secondly I put the cause down to money. If you want money for research these days, just mention climate change and you've got it. A number of big businesses are now also lining their pockets with environmental cash flowing from government coffers. Much of the rhetoric is now being driven by environmental industries that have massive vested interests in the climate change scenario.

Finally the climate change *con* is being driven by politics and self promotion. What kind of man runs for US president? An ambitious one of course!

Ladies and gentlemen the climate on earth is changing, it has always changed and it always will. The climate is the weather and weather changes nearly every day and we adapt. Let's get on with solving problems that we can do something about. There will be catastrophic climate changes in the future as there have been in the past, but they have nothing to do with man's activities. The debate is not over and there is no consensus!"

There was a round of applause from the small group and Jeff called for questions. One of the students asked "what if you're wrong and how can it hurt to take some action against climate change just in case?"

"The problem is cost" Jeff replied. "The proposed actions to "tackle" climate change will add to the cost of energy and therefore the cost of everything else. Increasing our costs means lowering our standard of living. Also if we make changes unilaterally or differently from other nations then we will also export jobs offshore."

"I can't believe we've all been so hoodwinked!" another student exclaimed.

"It does seem incredible," Jeff replied. "But when you think about it, environmentalism and climate change are very easy to sell. When someone says "you are stealing from your children" or "you are ruining the planet for future generations" this raises a good deal of emotion, guilt in particular. It doesn't have to be true to be effective."

Bill had been listening intently to Jeff's speech which he found fascinating. He had similar views about global warming but had not seen such a succinct case put before. Following the meeting he congratulated Jeff warmly for his excellent speech and asked if he could have a copy of it. Jeff willingly agreed but did not want it publicised with his name on it. He explained that he had been in some trouble before at the university over his views on climate change and had become wary.

Several days after the delivery of Jeff's speech to the science sceptics Bill had a knock on his door. Jeff stood there looking slightly annoyed and said "do you want to come and have a beer with me? I think I need one."

When they had settled down with a beer at the local hotel, Jeff proceeded to explain his troubles. Apparently one of the students that had been at the science sceptics meeting had told Jeff's supervisor about his speech. This had not gone down well, as Jeff's supervisor was an outspoken climate change advocate.

"I hope we haven't got you in too much trouble" Bill said with concern.

"No it's OK, it's been building up to this for some time anyway" Jeff replied. "My supervisor and I have had some serious conflicts from day one. My thesis concerns the affect of salinity on certain crops. When I project results into the future, he wants me to use climate models that predict all this CO_2 induced climate change nonsense. As you've gathered I have no time for these models. They are completely dependent on the assumptions you build into them and none of them can be made to fit past data. I've tried arguing about it, but it's become a stalemate and they just see me as a bloody heretic."

"And they're out to burn you at the stake too I expect" Bill sympathised.

"Yep and I've just about had a guts full of it. I need to rethink my whole future I reckon. I usually head up into the Snowy Mountains for some trout fishing when I want to think. Do you fancy coming with me this long weekend?" Jeff enquired.

"I'd love to" Bill replied enthusiastically. "I used to do a lot of fly fishing in my younger days back in New Zealand. I haven't fished for years but I still have all my gear. I have a friend who's an outdoors type, would you mind if I ask him to come along?" Bill had an ulterior motive in asking this question. He was keen for Aaron to meet Jeff.

They met Aaron at the Canberra airport, loaded their fishing gear and backpacks into a rental car and headed for the mountains. Jeff navigated them to a stretch of the river that was normally inaccessible to the public, but he had a longstanding arrangement with a local landowner. They drove along a bumpy narrow farm track to a point where they would need to hike the rest of the way. After loading up their backpacks they commenced the long walk through the bush to get to the river.

After quickly setting up camp by the river they couldn't wait to get into the fishing. Bill was surprised at how clear and fast-flowing the river was. It reminded him of a mountain stream in New Zealand. Jeff suggested that Bill and Aaron cover the stretch of the river close to the camp and he would walk further upstream and meet them back at the camp just before dark. Aaron had not been fly fishing before and Bill took it upon himself to teach him the skills. He felt quite proud to be the mentor for a change as Aaron was usually the teacher and he the apprentice.

Aaron was a fast learner and was soon casting his fly with adequate precision above the lie that Bill had suggested may house a trout. Bill was not that worried about catching a fish, he had caught many in his life. He just loved the peace and serenity of the surroundings. Moreover he was keen for Aaron to experience the fun of catching his first trout.

He sat on the bank offering Aaron advice now and then about where to cast and how to regather his line as the fly drifted back towards him. At one point he felt a sharp stinging pain in his thigh under his shorts and looked down to see a large ant, its pincers clinging into his flesh, it's body arched so that its sting drilled into his soft flesh. He leapt into the air brushing it off shouting "ouch bloody bull ant!"

Aaron roared with laughter at the sight of Bill leaping around like a madman on the bank "you Kiwi's aren't used to those big Aussie bulldog ants" he laughed.

Bill glared back at the unsympathetic Aaron as he rubbed the sting, only slowly regaining his sense of humour. "Yeah it's hard to get used to all the creepy crawlies over here" he muttered. "It always amazes me how many different kinds there are in Australia. Back in New Zealand there were no stinging or biting ants."

Aaron wasn't listening, he was cursing and grumbling as he had got his line into an extreme tangle; he had hooked the fly into his back and somehow got the line wound around himself several times. "Karmic justice" Bill chuckled as he went to help Aaron out of his predicament.

"Yeah, touché thanks for the help" Aaron replied sheepishly as Bill unwound the line and unhooked the fly from his back. "No stingers in New Zealand you say."

"Not as far as I know" Bill replied as he stepped back out of the stream allowing Aaron to continue casting. But isn't it amazing the way ants behave. It's mind-blowing how they all work as a team, with different jobs and so on. I've heard that the older ants get to do all the dangerous jobs."

"Yeah, unlike us who send our young fit men off to war" Aaron replied. "Bees are like that too. The colony works as a whole. We don't really understand how they do it, but it makes me laugh when I hear Darwinists say it's all come about by random chance."

"Me too I've been having some discussions with my supervisor Tim about Darwinism."

"Oh, what does he think?"

"Well he's traditionally been a Darwinist but I reckon he's starting to see the light" Bill replied.

"Is he a candidate for the Junto, do you think?"

"Maybe, but I think Jeff might be a more likely starter. What did you think of his speech?" Bill had given Aaron a copy.

"Pretty good, what does he think about God?" Aaron asked as he flicked his line back out.

"He's a bit confused, he has a problem rationalising how science and religion can exist together."

"That's pretty common among scientists with religious beliefs" Aaron responded. "They just seem to turn their brain off when they get to Church. They keep science and religion in separate compartments."

"That seems to be pretty much what Jeff does" Bill agreed.

"It's OK though, at least he's not an atheist and he seems very genuine" Aaron responded then suddenly he yelled "Yeehah!"

"Hold your rod up!" Bill shouted excitedly, "don't pull too hard, just play it gently, let it run." Aaron's reel screamed as the hapless trout raced downstream breaking the surface briefly before leaping completely out of the water revealing its full glistening splendour. Aaron played the fish for several minutes, obeying Bill's many instructions that finally resulted in a tired rainbow trout being dragged to the shallows so that Bill could flick it onto the stony shore.

"Congratulations she's a real beauty, a good four pounds I reckon" Bill said as he looked up to see Aaron's beaming face. He felt the pang of joy that accompanies the sharing in a friend's happiness and success. In his younger days he might have felt a tinge of jealousy on such an occasion, but not now. He had long since learned how to control this immature emotion. He watched as Aaron put the twitching fish out of its misery and gave him further instructions about cleaning it. "That's the fun part" Bill laughed as he showed Aaron the easy way to strip the guts from the trout.

In the excitement they hadn't noticed that it was getting late. "We'd better get back to the camp" Bill remarked. "I wouldn't want to be out here much longer. It would be a devil of a job getting back at night, it's a new moon."

"I wonder where Jeff is" Aaron said with concern.

"I'm sure he'll turn up" Bill replied. "He knows this area pretty well." They made their way quickly back to the camp as the shadows lengthened around them and darkness fell. They lit a hearty fire hoping that Jeff would see it.

Bill showed Aaron his favourite way of cooking a trout. He sliced the fish down the middle, sandwiched in some butter and lemon with a sprinkle of herbs and wrapped it in tinfoil before tossing it on the embers.

They were becoming increasingly anxious that Jeff hadn't returned, but both knew that there was little they could do. There was no mobile phone coverage in the area, Aaron did not have his satellite phone this time and they had forgotten to bring torches. "Maybe that yummy smell will bring him back" Bill said as he unwrapped the fish.

"Delicious" Aaron declared as he finished his portion of the fish. They left some for Jeff hoping he might still show up and got into their sleeping bags, planning a start at daybreak to look for him. Bill prayed silently that Jeff would be OK as he drifted into a patchy and restless sleep. It was autumn and already cold at this altitude.

He awoke before dawn to the sound of Aaron stoking the fire to boil the billy. They sipped their coffee in silence as the first light slowly started to descend into the valley. As they prepared to set off they were startled by a shout. They looked out through the gloomy shadows to see a bedraggled looking Jeff striding towards them.

"Where the hell have you been" Bill scolded "we've been worried sick!" Jeff was noticeably shivering all over but was grinning widely. Dangling from his belt was a huge trout.

"Sorry about that" Jeff stuttered. "I just need to get out of these wet clothes and I'll tell you what happened." Aaron stoked up the fire again as Jeff changed and gratefully accepted a steaming hot coffee.

"The main problem was I went further up the river than I intended and fished just a little bit too long. I caught this beauty just on dusk. As it got dark I thought I would just be able to follow the river back, but the rocks were too slippery and hard to negotiate. I stumbled and fell in at one stage, that's how I got wet. In the end I figured I'd be better off staying put until morning. I couldn't see a darn thing. I had this survival blanket in my pocket which was a real life saver, but it was a very long night."

"I'll bet it was" Bill sympathised.

Jeff slowly thawed out by the fire and despite protests from Bill and Aaron due to his continued shivering he said he would be fine to get back to the fishing. This time they decided to stick together, taking it in turns to fish the lies as they ambled down the stream. Bill did most of the fishing as he was the only one yet to catch one. They talked mostly about environmental issues as Jeff explained his predicament at university with his supervisors.

"It's not just the climate change issue" Jeff explained. "It's the whole environmentalist thing. I used to have some idealistic notions about saving the planet, but I've come to realise that the planet is just fine. When you look down into a smouldering crater of a volcano you realise that the Earth is just a big piece of rock that recycles itself without any help from us."

"You're dead right there" Aaron agreed. "Saving the planet is a ridiculous notion. It's only people that need saving. Many environmentalists have this idea that the planet can be preserved forever, but this is impossible. God gave us the planet for a certain limited amount of time to learn our lessons. Even if we could lengthen the life of the planet it would achieve nothing if we don't learn the lessons intended for us."

Jeff nodded, he had already begun to respect Aaron and, wanting to hear more, he remained silent.

Aaron continued "even the idea of preserving various animal species and so on is not helpful in the long run. Ninety-nine percent of all species that ever existed are already extinct without any influence from man. God's creatures come and go, but only mankind has the ability to master this existence. Unfortunately most in the environmental movement are atheists who believe that man is just an advanced ape in the animal kingdom. Another confounding problem is that it has become fashionable to be "caring" for the environment as if it were a virtue. So when the likes of Al Gore blatantly exaggerate and even downright lie about the evidence for human induced global warming it's considered acceptable because it's in a "good cause."

There's also a severely misguided element that imagine the world would be better off without humans. They don't understand that man is on a different level to animals and has been given a purpose. We must fight against this element that would have us return to the dark ages with its subsistence farming, inefficiency and barbarity. These fanatics operate by spreading fear and by making people feel guilty."

"I know where you're coming from there" Jeff remarked. "My faculty is full of those types. But isn't there a valid argument that our natural resources are limited and we need to manage them responsibly so as not to deprive future generations of them?"

"Certainly, some of our resources are limited and reasonable recycling is a good thing but, generally speaking, free market pricing will ensure the supply of our resources. In a free market economy the price of a particular resource increases as the availability decreases and innovative people will eventually find a more economic alternative. The basic flaw in conservationists' logic is that our use of resources will continue until they run out. This is not the case, we keep making better use of resources as they become scarce and we start to use alternatives when the price gets to a certain point. We will even recycle when it becomes economic to do so" Aaron grinned.

Jeff nodded, "are there any environmental issues then that we ought to be genuinely concerned about do you think?"

"Yes indeed there are many localised environmental issues that are valid concerns especially in developing nations. In civilised wealthy nations problems such as air and water pollution have largely been addressed. Remember that environmentalism is only feasible in wealthy countries so we must maintain a strong economy if we want to be clean and green."

"You've just about convinced me I'm wasting my time in environmental science" Jeff sighed.

"Sorry, I am inclined to be tactless" Aaron sympathised "but the work you're doing on salinity is a very real problem."

"Thanks, but it's all the other bullshit I have to deal with" Jeff muttered.

Bill had been listening to the conversation as best he could over the noise of the running water when suddenly he felt the faint tug of the line that he knew so well. He flicked his rod skilfully setting the hook firmly and the next ten minutes were all action with Aaron and Jeff yelling encouragement. When Bill had landed his trout they decided to head for home. Jeff was still shivering and they thought he would need a night in a warm bed to fully recover.

Chapter 4 - Organics

"What reason weaves, by passion is undone" Alexander Pope

After the fishing trip Bill decided to approach Hillary regarding her offer of some tutorial work to help with her organics class. Bill had completed research for his Master of Science comparing certain aspects of organic agriculture with conventional methods and he was therefore quite well qualified to assist.

His interest in organics had started years before when he had become concerned about the high use of some agricultural chemicals in vineyards and wanted to minimise their use in his own. However the findings from his research had made him somewhat disillusioned with organics. He found that much of what he had originally thought worthwhile in organic agriculture had now been taken up by mainstream agriculture. For example the concept of "sustainability" was now embraced by modern conventional farmers.

He also found that claims by the organic food industry that their product was healthier or of better quality are largely unfounded and unproven at best. Chemical residues in western nations are regulated so that all food is relatively safe whether organically produced or not. The "Fable for Tomorrow" chapter in Rachel Carson's 1962 book "Silent Spring" that helped to spawn the organic industry had not eventuated. Quite the opposite had actually occurred, with people now living longer and healthier lives and food production was now dramatically higher.

Furthermore Bill found that some of the chemicals that were allowed to be used by organic growers because they were considered to be "natural" were doing more harm than their conventional rivals. Because organic growers are not permitted to use herbicides, they also tended to overly rely on cultivation which may be degrading the soil.

Moreover, the main disadvantage of organic agriculture he had found was its lower productivity and higher cost. In most cases organic enterprises were small and could not compete in the modern world that requires high production, efficiency and economies of scale. Bill suspected that organics was ironically *less* sustainable in the long term because of a run down in the nutritional status of some organic properties owing to the higher cost of supplying organic fertilisers.

At the administrative and marketing level the organic industry was a shambles because of the lack of a widely accepted definition of organics and uniform standards. The large number of organic certifiers with different standards and marketing brands caused confusion in the marketplace worldwide.

Despite Bill's many reservations however, he believed that there were some useful practices that can be learned from organic agriculture and applied to the conventional industry. These included cultural practices, better monitoring for disease and the use of mulches to improve soil qualities. There also seemed to be a niche market for organic produce particularly in Europe. However this market was difficult to access by growers outside Europe owing to internal subsidies and the growing concern about "food miles."

These thoughts were running through Bill's mind as he explained his previous research to Hillary. He kept most of his negative views about organics to himself because he knew she was a "believer" and would not listen to anything critical. He only briefly alluded to his findings. He was reasonably confident that she would not read his thesis because she showed little interest when he started to explain it. In fact she didn't seem to be listening to any of what he said.

Hillary was however friendly in spite of the initial conflict in the tearoom. She explained that she had got behind with her marking and was grateful for the chance to delegate it and asked if Bill would also like to take over the tutorial sessions in organic agriculture.

Bill readily agreed to the work as it was a much needed source of income. "Here you can start with this" Hillary smiled as she gave him a huge pile of marking.

When he sat down to mark the assignments he was horrified to see that they were well overdue to be handed back. He worked late over several nights to complete it.

At the first organics tutorial session Bill was approached by one of the students who complained to him about Hillary. "She's lazy and never marks stuff on time" the student complained. "Her lectures are a waste of time; I wish I'd never taken this unit."

"Those are strong words" Bill replied, shocked at the strength of the outburst, but not very surprised at the criticism.

"Yes but its true, ask anyone in the class" the student responded emphatically.

Bill subtly gained feedback from other students in the class to corroborate the complaint. From his investigations it seemed that the complaint was no exaggeration. Several students even complained that they had some assignments "go missing" after submission to Hillary. They had received passing grades for the work but never had it returned to them despite repeated requests to Hillary.

The situation put Bill in a rather awkward position. Because he was new he did not want to rock the boat. He tried to broach the missing assignments issue with Hillary but she merely shrugged her shoulders and said that the students must have lost them or they went missing in the post. Bill decided not to take the issue any further because the only other person he could go to was Professor Natal and he didn't want to do that. Instead he decided to help the students where he could and to keep an eye on Hillary. In any case he was now doing most of the marking. Hillary was supposed to review it but did not.

One day he went to drop off some marking to Hillary. Her door was closed so he knocked and went in. He gasped with surprise at the sight in front of him. Hillary was locked hand in hand with three people, one man and two other women. They were all chanting in low voices and sitting around a Ouija Board.

"Don't you know how to bloody knock?" Hillary hissed as she looked up and stopped chanting.

"Oh sorry" Bill replied. "I did actually knock; I didn't mean to disturb you."

Hillary stared at him momentarily then changed her tone. "Oh that's OK we're just doing some channelling here. This is my husband Pete and this is Heidi and Jessica. We are trying to contact their mother who died recently."

"Pleased to meet you" Bill stammered, still struggling to comprehend the scene. He excused himself again for interrupting and left.

Later that day Hillary phoned Bill requesting a meeting. She seemed rather anxious as he sat down in her office. "I just wanted to explain a few things about what you saw earlier" she began.

"You mean the séance?" Bill asked.

"Yes, you obviously know something about it. I found out a few years ago that I was clairvoyant" Hillary replied.

"What does that mean?"

"It means I can talk to people on the "other side" in the spirit world."

"Oh" Bill responded. "Isn't that a bit dangerous?"

"What do you mean?" Hillary sounded irritated.

"Well it's just that I've heard about people developing mental illness through delving into the spirit world."

"That's bullshit" she replied indignantly.

Bill decided not to pursue this line; instead he asked "how did you get into spiritualism?"

Hillary replied "well it started with biodynamic agriculture, how much do you know about that?"

"A little" Bill responded. "It's a branch of organic agriculture that's based on the teachings of Rudolf Steiner. I came across it in my studies and wanted to investigate it but the biodynamic association wasn't interested in being part of my study."

"That's a shame; you'd think they would welcome scientific investigation. I know for a fact that it works. It's very popular in Europe and it's taking off here in a big way."

"Tell me how it works" Bill suggested.

"OK I'll try, but I'd better give you some background first. You see Rudolf Steiner was a philosopher who gained his insights through direct contact with the spirit world and the Akashic record."

"What do you mean by Akashic record?" Bill had a fair idea what this was about but wanted to hear Hillary's interpretation.

"The Akashic record is where all the history of mankind is stored. It's on the etheric level of existence and only clairvoyant people can see it."

"Can you see it?" Bill asked.

"Err not exactly," Hillary replied hesitantly "but I can hear spirits who are ascended masters and they tell me things that are on the Akashic record. Anyway to continue, Steiner formed the anthroposophy movement which now runs Waldorf schools and biodynamic agriculture was created from a series of Steiner lectures to a group of German farmers."

"What's the basis of it?"

"Well it assumes the whole farm is a living entity, that plants have a spirit world and that we can tap into that spirit world through biodynamic practices."

"What are biodynamic practices?"

"It mostly revolves around various preparations, the main ones being 500 and 501. Preparation 500 is cow manure buried in a cow horn for a year and preparation 501 is ground silica or quartz. But also it involves doing certain practices according to phases of the moon and sometimes planetary cycles."

"Sounds a bit like astrology" Bill suggested.

"Perhaps, Steiner was also an astrologer, as am I" Hillary responded proudly.

"I have my reservations about astrology" Bill said politely, though he would like to have put it much more strongly. He had long believed that astrology was absurd and that it's implication that people were a certain way owing to the alignment of stars and planets was ludicrous.

"Well" Hillary replied, "it doesn't really matter whether you believe it or not. I just know that it works."

"How do you know that it works?"

"There are lots of big producers who are using it in Europe."

"But how do you know that the preparations and the moon cycles and so on are responsible?"

At this point Hillary became angry and raised her voice. "Look the proof is in the bloody pudding OK!"

"Sure, I'm sorry" Bill said quietly, "but getting back to the spiritualism, how did you get into that?"

"It's all part of it. In for a penny in for a pound! I started to study anthroposophy and one thing lead to another until I found that I could tap into the spirit world quite easily myself."

"How do you know the information you are getting from the spirit world is accurate?" Bill enquired.

"Because I only call up higher beings or masters, who we can always rely on" Hillary responded now getting highly agitated.

"But how do you know that the spirits you're talking to are really who they say they are? They might be just an evil spirit pretending to be good like a wolf in sheep's clothing."

Hillary banged her fist on the table and shouted "no, no they aren't allowed to do that!"

Bill felt an uncomfortable chill in the air and noticed that Hillary's eyes had become dark. He thought he had better not go any further with this. "OK, I'm sorry" he said "I didn't mean to offend you I'm just curious. Was there anything else you wanted to see me about?" Hillary shook her head and Bill was grateful to hear a knock at the door and a student came in.

Bill was glad that he was due to go home for the weekend soon after this conversation and could forget about the unpleasantness. As usual Sarah greeted him lovingly and they proceeded to catch up on each other's news. Sarah had prepared a wonderful dinner for Bill. At one point during the meal Bill asked about one of the ingredients in the meal and made a rather negative remark about it. This was out of character for him, Sarah was an excellent cook and Bill was normally very complimentary about her cooking.

Unfortunately Sarah took this comment badly. She had been looking forward to having Bill home again and had put a lot of effort into the meal. It was very stressful for her coping on her own with Bill away and this was like the straw that broke the camel's back. She snapped back at him, saying he could cook the damned thing himself next time. Bill, tired after a long drive and also under some stress, responded in kind. It soon developed into a full blown argument such as they hadn't had for years. They both screamed at each other, almost coming to blows as all rationality ceased. The taunts started to fly in both directions as all the petty irritations of nearly a lifetime together were thrown at each other. The sparring deteriorated into snide remarks such as "you're just like your mother."

Bill finally decided he could not take any more and stormed out the door, jumped in the car and drove off. He didn't know where he was going; he just knew he had to get away. After some deep breathing he slowly started to calm down and his mind began to clear. He stopped at the local McDonalds, went in and ordered a coffee.

Bill was ruminating on the conflict with Sarah staring into his coffee when he heard a voice. "Problems?" He looked up and to his surprise Hamish was standing there chuckling at the startled expression on Bill's face.

"You'll have to stop creeping up on me like this" Bill said. Though warmly shook Hamish's hand. "What are you doing here?"

"Coincidence" Hamish smiled mischievously. "But let's talk about you, you don't look very happy."

Bill explained the argument with Sarah to Hamish and said he didn't know why he had let it get so out of hand.

"And how is university going?" Bill was disappointed that Hamish did not offer him any advice about his argument with Sarah. As he explained the situation with Hillary, Hamish nodded attentively and seemed keenly interested when Bill told him about the conversation on biodynamic agriculture and spiritualism.

"That could be your problem right there" Hamish said. "You did right to confront Hillary about these things but unfortunately you have unleashed the wrath of some nasty entities."

"You mean evil spirits? Aaron has told me about them."

"Yes, I'm sure he has. You are correct that you can't trust the spirits are who they pretend to be. With information that has been divined there is no way of knowing where or from whom it came. There are no "contacts" with good beings through the methods used by spiritualists. Some of the real nasties can manifest themselves to the unwary as great ones, even as Jesus, the Virgin Mary or ascended masters."

"Hillary talked about ascended masters" Bill interrupted.

"Well there are indeed masters or we could call them saints that have mastered the human experience, but the entities Hillary has been contacting are definitely not masters. Sadly the evil ones are gaining more power through the practices of naive "New Age" people like Hillary. There are some very evil entities that seek to manipulate the minds of other people and lead them along a path to self destruction and our civilisation into chaos. Unfortunately there are some unsuspecting and even well intentioned people that are playing right into the hands of these entities."

"You hinted that there could be a connection between my confrontation with Hillary and my argument with Sarah?" Bill asked.

"Almost certainly" Hamish replied emphatically. "Your altercation with Hillary is not just with her. Because she is a willing medium, she provides a portal into our world and the means by which these malevolent beings may interfere in our affairs. Consequently there may be one or more of these entities more or less constantly hanging around her. They will now see you as a threat and will try to disrupt you in any way they can. You must be extremely vigilant that you do not give them the opportunity."

"How do I do that?" Bill asked apprehensively.

"First of all you must avoid any negative, hateful or fearful thoughts. When your argument with Sarah started to get out of hand your thoughts became hateful and this puts them on rapport with your mind and gives them strength. Once they gain a foothold they can even start to play tricks on your mind. In extreme situations it might even make you temporarily insane, whereby you lose control of your mind to them."

"It sounds pretty scary."

"Yes but do not fear, the evil ones cannot gain the upper hand unless you allow them to. Above all you must have faith in God and know that good always prevails over evil in the end. If you feel yourself sinking into negative or fearful thinking, immediately change your thoughts. This may not be easy. You may first of all need to distract yourself, for example by changing your immediate environment."

"You mean like I fled away from Sarah earlier?"

"Yes, that was probably the best thing to do under the circumstances, but of course you will now have to make up with her and get your relationship back on track."

"Absolutely, I'll phone her soon and apologise, I feel like a right bastard for some of the things I said to her and I didn't mean any of them."

"She will get over it" Hamish said sympathetically. "Your love for each other is strong and your relationship can survive much worse than this."

"Thanks for explaining all this to me Hamish. Underneath I guess I already know a lot about what you've been telling me. Aaron has told me about this sort of thing before. It's just that even when I know it sometimes I can't seem to help myself. I guess it's my old habits of thinking that die hard."

"Yes, habits do take a lot of work to change, but when things get really tough we may need to ask for help."

"Do you mean pray?" Bill asked.

Hamish nodded "now getting back to this biodynamic nonsense..."

"I'm glad you agree with me" Bill interrupted.

"Of course, when you consider that the source of the information is divination from the spirit world by Steiner and others it cannot possibly be relied upon. Essentially it's a pile of superstitious mumbo jumbo. There's a very good reason that the biodynamic organisation didn't want you to investigate them scientifically.

Mind you, there is some truth contained in the philosophies of theosophy and Steiner's anthroposophy. The problem is that it's impossible for most people to discern what's truth and what's garbage. When you read the ramblings of spiritualists such as Blavatsky and Steiner you'll see that it is by and large inconsistent, incoherent and incomprehensible."

"Is their anything positive in biodynamic agriculture then?" Bill asked.

"The practices of biodynamic agriculture in themselves are harmless enough and some may even be beneficial. The problem though is that it leads farmers away from modern production techniques that are an essential part of our modern well fed civilisation. Moreover there is something much more sinister at the heart of the biodynamic movement stemming from the evil that spawned it."

"Does this have something to do with the Nazis?" Bill interrupted.

"It is related" Hamish nodded. "You are aware that modern theosophy grew from the works of Helena Blavatsky who claimed that her insights came from Tibetan masters or mahatmas as she called them. In particular she refers to the "masters" Morya and Koothumi who had astral bodies and spoke to her telepathically. We have already discussed how these are nothing more than mischievous and malevolent entities who pretend to be saintly higher beings. A primary objective of these evil beings is to install an "antichrist" into a powerful position of leadership in the world. Steiner refers to this antichrist as the "Maitreya" who will supposedly come from Shamballah which is held by theosophy to be a hidden subterranean city beneath the Himalayas.

In the 1930s the Nazi's sent missions to Tibet to look for Shamballah and its sister city Agarthi as well as to trace their Aryan heritage by investigating the racial characteristics of the Tibetan people. Racism is a key tenet of Steiner's anthroposophy and is similar to the Nazi's racial ideology. Steiner believed that souls reincarnate and pass through racial stages with African and Asian races being lower than Europeans and of course his own Germanic-Nordic race (deriving from the Aryans) at the top. The Nazi ideology of the Aryan master race and the extermination of so-called inferior races came from these roots as well as from neo-Darwinism.

Steiner split with theosophy owing to a disagreement with its then leaders Annie Besant and C.W. Leadbetter who wished to declare a certain young man to be the reincarnated messiah. He formed his anthroposophy schism which purported to be a Christianised version of theosophy. The schism though has essentially the same philosophies and source as its parent philosophy.

The modern manifestation of this ideology is the "New Age" movement spawned by Alice Bailey, a medium who also claimed to channel and receive occult letters from a Tibetan master. More recently Benjamin Creme and others have continued this unholy alliance with the dark forces of mankind. Do you now understand the dangers of this movement Bill?"

"Pretty scary stuff. Are you sure about these things?"

"As sure as one can be about anything. But don't worry and above all do not fear. If you feel things are getting out of hand just pray for help. By the way how's the Junto coming along?"

"I'm starting to make progress I have one definite candidate and another strong possibility."

"That's great, keep up the good work. Now I'd better let you go so you can sort things out with Sarah."

"Thanks Hamish" Bill replied as they shook hands and Hamish left.

Bill phoned Sarah, apologised sincerely and she forgave him urging him to come home.

Chapter 5 - Evolution

"The scientific community is a pack of hounds where the louder-voiced bring many to follow them nearly as often in a wrong path as in a right one, where the entire pack even has been known to move bodily on a false scent" Samuel P Langley

After the second meeting of the science sceptics an attractive looking woman perhaps in her mid thirties had approached Bill and asked if she could present the talk for the next meeting on the subject of Intelligent Design. Bill readily agreed and accepted her request to move future meetings indoors to allow PowerPoint presentations.

A gathering of about twenty people assembled in the small lecture theatre that Bill had secured. Marion was dressed in a smart business suit and with her long brown hair falling neatly onto her shoulders Bill thought she looked stunning as she opened her speech.

"My talk today is about the highly controversial subject of Intelligent Design. I feel privileged to be able to address such an open minded group. I am a high school science teacher and I could not have given this speech at my school. In fact I was sacked from my position for merely pointing out an error in a text book that implied Darwin's theory of evolution is a fact.

First of all how many people know what Intelligent Design means?"

Marion strode forward and extended her arms inviting her audience to respond. A young man in the front asked if it had something to do with teaching creationism in schools.

"Well that's one way of putting it" Marion responded, "but we must be very specific about what we're talking about here. When people hear the word creationism they usually imagine the Genesis version of creation which is still popular with fundamentalist sects, but to the educated thinking person it is an inadequate explanation except in an allegorical sense. Critics like to use this word to imply that the ID movement is trying to teach religion in school science classes. That is not true. ID is *not* about religion. It's an alternative scientific theory to Darwinism. So let's avoid the word "creation" and stick to the word "design.""

Marion had become animated and beamed with enthusiasm. Bill noticed what seemed to be a golden glow of energy radiating outward from her head. He had occasionally noticed this phenomenon before when great speakers became impassioned by their subject matter.

"Let's get this perfectly clear. ID is not a debate about whether evolution is true or not. It's only an argument about the *means* of evolution. Did you and I get here by random chance, as Darwin believed or are we here by design? Now, who can explain to me briefly Darwin's theory of evolution?"

Another young man responded "I guess it's that chance genetic mutations are the cause of evolution. When a chance mutation occurs that makes a creature better adapted to its environment it will be more likely to survive. Thus the fittest mutation will survive and will pass on its genes to its offspring."

"Yes that's it in a nutshell" Marion complimented. "The key point is that Darwin's theory requires us to accept that it all happens by random chance. But is it reasonable to accept this? Is it sensible to believe that molecules assembled themselves by pure chance into you and me - the thinking, loving and beautiful beings that we are? To me believing in Darwinism is like believing an explosion in the wrecker's yard can result in a jumbo jet."

She paused for this message to sink in.

"I put it to you that you don't have to accept it, because it's *only a theory*! Darwin's theory of evolution is not a fact. It's a popular theory but popularity doesn't make it true. Until a few hundred years ago the most popular theory was that the earth is the centre of the solar system, but that didn't make it true. Sometimes I even wonder if Darwinism is a religion the way I hear it being preached with such fanatical zeal" Marion smiled.

"Darwin's theory says that each species has evolved from another species. But guess what? This has never been observed, not even in the fossil record. There is not one single case of evidence of one species evolving into another, even with bacteria that can have a new generation in half a day. After observing thousands of generations of E. coli bacteria, an E. coli is still an E. coli. But I don't want to dwell too much on this issue because it makes no difference to our topic whether one species has been evolved from another. We are here to talk about whether it all happens by chance or by design.

What gets in the way of the truth when we talk about these issues is dogma, both religious and science dogma. For a start religious dogma is a problem. Some people see the Bible, the Koran, the Torah or other religious text as an absolute authority. Because of this view they cannot accept anything that contradicts this absolute "Truth."" Marion stabbed the inverted commas into the air pointedly with her fingers. "This is a real handicap for them. On the other hand most scientists have thrown the baby out with the bath water. Because some of the specific historical claims of the Bible have been disproved, they feel they're entitled to toss the whole thing out. It's an all or nothing kind of thing on both sides. But we don't need to do this.

Don't get me wrong, I'm not against religion, far from it. I'm just in favour of Truth. We sometimes forget that science itself arose in a Christian society. It didn't arise out of an atheist society. Many people who have made the greatest scientific discoveries have been devout Christians: Galileo, Kepler, Newton and Boyle to name a few. Even Einstein could see the value of religion. He wrote and I quote: "science without religion is lame, religion without science is blind."

Unfortunately, or fortunately you might say" Marion chuckled, "religion no longer plays any part in science. Interestingly though we've made very few scientific discoveries since Einstein except in the field of genetics.

Having discredited religion, science has now developed its own dogma. We could write it down as follows." Marion clicked her computer into action and projected the following onto the screen:

The Science Dogma

- There is no God – atheism is the rational view of existence
- All creatures evolved via random chance genetic mutations
- People are merely more evolved animals
- Beyond this physical life there is nothing
- The only objective for humans is to maximise pleasure and minimise pain
- Religion is a myth invented either to comfort or to control people

"If we accept this dogma then our lives have no more purpose or meaning than that of a fly. What's more is that the atheist is a dangerous creature because she believes in no power greater than herself and her highest aspiration is the fulfilment of her own ego. With this view of reality we can rationalise any cruel and vicious behaviour we like. We could even justify the Nazi agenda. Why don't we just cull the inferior people?

Well I don't accept the Science Dogma and for the next part of my talk I'll show you six good reasons why you don't have to accept it either. You will see why ID is a valid scientific theory and when you consider it with an open mind you may conclude that it's a more logical and rational view than Darwinism."

Marion paused again to bring up another slide on the screen. Bill looked around the audience to gauge their level of interest and saw that they were mostly riveted, as he was himself. Her next slide was headed "Irreducible complexity" and showed a picture of the flagellum for the E. coli bacteria. Bill was aware that this fascinating propulsion system had become something of an icon for the Intelligent Design movement.

Marion continued "Darwin wrote that if it could be demonstrated that any complex organ existed which could not possibly have been formed by numerous successive, slight modifications, his theory would absolutely break down. Well guess what, this appears to be a prime example of such an organ.

The flagellum is like a little outboard motor and consists of several complex parts. If we take away any one of these parts then the whole thing is useless. There are no interim stages from which this system could have evolved."

Marion reached into her bag and pulled out a mouse trap. "Michael Behe is a great advocate for the ID movement and he has explained irreducible complexity using a mousetrap analogy. If you take away any one of these parts the whole thing is useless. None of the individual parts on their own is of any use, nor any combination of the parts except the complete package. So we can't explain an evolutionary path that would assemble all these parts bit by bit through various chance mutations to get the complete and final item.

My second argument is about the nature of DNA." Marion showed a drawing of the DNA molecule and explained how it was a code just like the one we use to program computers, though more complex. "DNA is the software but software requires a designer, codes don't just write themselves!" she exclaimed passionately. This reminded Bill of his talk with Tim. She could be taking the words right out of my mouth, he thought.

"Argument number three is about human evolution." Marion's next slide was a picture of a chimpanzee dressed up in formal clothes wearing horn-rimmed spectacles and apparently reading a copy of Tolstoy's "War and Peace."

"We have ninety-eight percent the same DNA as this chimp." She then showed a slide of a cocker spaniel similarly dressed and apparently reading the same book. "But we only have about sixty percent the same DNA as this spaniel. But it looks to me like the dog and the chimp have a lot more in common with each other than with us. I mean we're flying spaceships to Mars and these guys are just sitting around reading War and Peace." Chuckles came from the audience.

"You may laugh but it really is that silly to believe that the only difference between us and our furry friends is a few strands of DNA. To me it's as plain as the light of day that we have certain qualities that are well above and beyond the animal. Try reasoning with your dog. Rational thinking has evolved only once. On the other hand flight has supposedly evolved four times and vision forty times. How can that be?"

Marion smiled and winked at Bill. Has she read my book? Bill wondered as he remembered presenting a similar argument there.

"My fourth argument concerns free will" Marion declared. "If the atheist position is taken to its logical conclusion, humans have no free will, because we're merely complex animals whose behaviour is solely determined by our DNA, which is in turn derived from random evolution, right? This "fact" is the only logical conclusion one can draw from the chance evolution dogma and yet this defies all logic."

Marion pulled out a hair pin and said "I might just stab myself with this pin. Shall I do it or not? Will I, won't I. Oh I'd better do it, what the hell I'll just go ahead and stab myself shall I? My DNA is telling me to do it." Some of the audience giggled. "No, I'm sorry" Marion quipped, "the idea that we have no free will is that ridiculous.

This is a real problem for the atheists. They cannot explain free will. In fact free will isn't possible under their theory and yet free will is at the heart of our society. Without free will there is no such thing as morality. If we have no free will we can't be held accountable for our actions. I'm not guilty your honour my genes made me rob the bank. Actually most people accept that humans have free will without even realising it. Our laws and notions of personal responsibility are built on this premise.

Related to this is the "problem" of evil. People sometimes say to me there can't be a God because if there was He wouldn't allow evil in the world. But if we've been designed to have free will we therefore have the ability to *choose* evil. It's not God that has created evil but man. And why do we have free will? Maybe it's so we can learn from our mistakes.

Argument number five is about probability and the burden of proof. Is it more plausible that we happened by chance or that we were designed? Which theory is the more rational? Which has the highest mathematical probability? Well I'm no mathematician but I've been informed that the probability that it all came together by chance is such that there would not be enough time in the universe to make it happen.

And why is the burden of proof always on the ID movement to prove their case? The Darwinist atheist theory assumes their position of authority but we've seen that their theory is perhaps less likely than ID.

My final argument is how do we explain that order has come from chaos? The natural physical laws of the universe tend towards entropy or chaos; we see this in our everyday observations as well as at the quantum level. Natural laws tend towards chaos and yet there is order in "creation." Where does order come from if not from a designer? Where does life come from in the first place and the energies that form the universe?

So those are the six arguments and if I haven't convinced you of the validity of ID I hope I have at least convinced you not to shut your minds to the theory of ID. It's not religion it's an alternative scientific theory. If we fail to present this theory in schools we are failing not just our students but the future of mankind. And even if both theories are just as likely to be true, would you rather believe in hope and faith or would you rather hang on to the empty philosophy of Nietzsche, Stalin and Richard Dawkins, that life is without meaning?" Marion ended her talk with this open question and asked for questions from the floor.

A member of the audience asked "why do you think guys like Dawkins are so fixed in their views?"

Marion responded "Richard Dawkins is no different from other fundamentalists in the way he clings to his beliefs. We need to remember that atheism is also a "faith." One can't disprove that God exists any more than one can prove that He does. The problem with guys like Dawkins is the passion with which he holds his beliefs and how this passion is used to cajole others. The more passionately one holds onto one's beliefs the harder it is to accept any criticism of them. Unfortunately the strength of someone's opinion is not a good indicator of Truth. Hitler, Stalin and Osama Bin Laden were all convinced they were right. Even if Dawkins could see flaws in his pigheaded arguments he could not admit he is wrong. He's invested too much in his position, his career and written too many books on the subject. He cannot retreat because saving face has become the driving force to preserve the ego. And of course when you have no God you have no need for humility."

After the final applause and thanks Bill complemented Marion on her remarkable, thought provoking speech and invited her to discuss it over a coffee.

Marion smiled a little nervously as they sat down in the canteen, "I hope you didn't mind too much that I plagiarised a little from your book about the chimpanzee analogy."

Bill smiled "not a problem, it's the ideas that are important, not who came up with them. There's nothing new under the sun anyway. I'm just glad to hear that someone's read my book. It's hardly an academic work."

"I know that but I really did love it" Marion replied excitedly. "I actually stumbled on your book just before I lost my job."

"Oh dear, I hope that wasn't the reason you lost your job!" Bill exclaimed.

"Heavens no, but when I saw your name on the flyer about the science sceptics I put two and two together and got really inspired to present a talk to your group. I'm so rapt to meet you in person. When I read your book it was like I'd read it before or I was coming home or something. The ideas rang so true to me."

"Well thank you Marion" Bill beamed with delight. He was unaccustomed to such praise. "I was likewise impressed with your speech. Where did you get your material to put up such a well presented case?"

"I've been following the whole ID movement for a while and have seen it grow from small beginnings" she replied.

"I thought the way you presented your material in a scientific and well reasoned way was wonderful. I've seen the case for ID put before but usually it's being argued by a fundamentalist Christian who has their own agenda. When they talk about trying to prove the earth is only six thousand years old or something equally ridiculous they blow the whole thing away."

"I know what you mean" Marion agreed. "I'm a science teacher and can't ignore all my scientific training, but equally I can't ignore what I feel about the evidence for God and the lack of evidence for Darwinism. Of course that's what got me into trouble."

"You mean how you got the sack for pointing out an error in the text book."

"Yes, but to be honest, there was a bit more to it than that" Marion confessed. "It was really quite a build up. You see I used to have discussions in the school staff room with my colleagues about ID and I guess I developed a reputation for being a bit outspoken. While I never took ID into the class room, I did point out to my students that the text was wrong to imply that Darwin's theory of evolution by natural selection was a fact. One of the students told their parents about it and they took it to the school principal. He more or less forced me to resign to save a big stink at the school. I wasn't really worried because I'd been planning to take a year's leave to do this Graduate Diploma course anyway."

"What about when you're ready to go back" Bill asked "won't it be a problem?"

"Oh sure I'd have a problem going back into the public system" Marion replied "but I'm sure I'll be scooped up by a private Christian school especially when I've got my Graduate Diploma."

"I'm sure you will, what are you studying?"

"Would you believe Intelligent Design?"

"No, not really."

"Well you'd be right" Marion smiled "I'm actually studying evolutionary biology."

"Wow isn't that like going to bed with the enemy? How do you do your assignments when you know there's so much nonsense in it?"

"No problem, you just have to play the game, tell them what they want to hear. You can't always say what you think you know."

"You're right there" Bill nodded.

"But even when you have to write it up a certain way to keep them happy you can still study the research data with an open mind, I love the field of enquiry and trying to sort out fact from fiction."

"You're a very brave young lady and charming too" Bill gushed.

They locked eyes and the moment became slightly awkward. Marion appeared to blush as she said "actually I'm not as young as you might think."

"There's a College function on tonight. Would you like to come along with me and we can continue our discussion?" Bill asked hesitantly.

"I'd love to" Marion responded, her smile returning.

The function was a formal affair and Bill was dressed in a dinner suit as he greeted Marion. "Wow you look lovely" he said admiring her pretty black dress.

"You scrub up pretty well yourself" she replied "you look a totally different man."

They found a table where they could talk more or less in private and became engrossed in each other's stories. Bill was oblivious to the surroundings as Marion told him her life story. She had been married for many years but she and her husband had failed to have children and had eventually drifted apart. Marion's husband had remarried and now had his own family. Marion had since devoted herself to her work and felt that she was fulfilling her maternal instincts by being a good teacher. Bill was able to glean from her story that she was now about thirty-nine.

Bill reciprocated by telling Marion much about his own life and found himself explaining rather more than he should have at this early stage about his mission concerning the Junto. She was fascinated and said she would love to be part of it. "I think I've found my next candidate" he said as he looked into her bright blue eyes. "My God you look like a movie star and you have the mind of a genius, you're gorgeous" he blurted.

Marion looked taken aback and he immediately regretted his outburst. There was an uncomfortable silence until Marion finally replied "from what you've told me you're happily married to a woman you love very much. You're a very interesting man but I could never get involved with a married man. I think you might have been away from your wife for too long."

"I'm sorry" he stammered. "I had no right, I'm sorry I must have drunk too much wine."

"That's OK, no harm done, its getting quite late though and I'd like to get to bed" Marion replied.

Bill continued to feel embarrassed about his behaviour and when he saw Marion again the following day, he repeated his apology and said he would still like her to meet Aaron with a view to joining the Science Junto. He consequently invited her home to his vineyard for the weekend if he could arrange for Aaron to join them. Marion agreed as long as he didn't think it was too much trouble for his wife.

Aaron was also agreeable, saying he would be delighted to meet Marion and looked forward also to seeing Bill's vineyard and to finally meet Sarah. Sarah proved to be a little more difficult, perhaps it was because she sensed something in Bill's voice. She did however eventually agree to the weekend on the grounds that Aaron needed to meet this woman to assess her suitability for the Junto. She knew everything about Bill's project and had promised to be supportive.

It was all arranged for the following weekend and Marion seemed very excited and bubbly when Bill picked her up on the Friday afternoon. She appeared to have forgotten all about the previous embarrassment and it seemed there was no longer any awkwardness between them. Throughout the drive they were engrossed in deep philosophical discussion about some of the issues Bill had covered in his book and about the relationship between science and religion.

The journey seemed to go really quickly and they soon found themselves exchanging greetings with Sarah who was very polite as she welcomed Marion and showed her to her room. When she got Bill alone she scolded him for not telling her how pretty Marion was. "I hope you haven't been making an idiot of yourself" she said, knowing full well that Bill had a weakness for attractive intelligent women. Bill had never been unfaithful to

Sarah, but there were times when she felt that she needed to rein him in and remind him of the boundaries of her rightful territory. Bill was a little sheepish in his self defence but assured Sarah this was a purely professional association. He saw the fire in Sarah's eyes and he remembered why he had married her in the first place and realised how much he loved her, his best friend and devoted wife.

Sarah accepted Bill's explanation and they settled down to have dinner. Aaron wasn't due to arrive until the following morning and the cosy threesome initially created quite an awkward atmosphere. As the evening wore on however Sarah seemed to warm to Marion and they became increasingly engaged in conversation. They talked a great deal about education in which they shared a common passion. When finally they started to talk about subjects that are only interesting to women Bill began to feel so left out that he excused himself and went to bed. As he was drifting off to sleep he heard Sarah come to bed and he pretended not to hear when she said "she *is* lovely."

In the morning Aaron arrived and after initial introductions there were smiles, conversation and good humour all round. In the afternoon Bill and Sarah enjoyed showing off their vineyard and then they all went on a long bush walk.

Aaron had brought some venison steaks from one of his hunting expeditions and Bill cooked them on the barbeque for the evening meal while having a beer with Aaron. "What do you think?" Bill asked. This was the first time Bill had been able to talk to Aaron alone as the women were now inside chatting while Sarah cooked the vegetables.

"She's amazing" Aaron replied "how did you find her?"

"She found me, serendipity or something. Maybe it's that phenomenon we've talked about where minds with shared thoughts are mutually attracted by forces we don't understand."

"You could be right" Aaron concluded. There was quite a long silence before the conversation moved on and they talked about more trivial matters. There was no further mention about Marion.

"Those steaks smell delicious" Sarah said as they sat down to dine. There were compliments all around and Marion raved that Bill and Sarah's wine was also divine.

During dinner Aaron opened up about his past, revealing a side of him that Bill had not seen before. He explained that he had once been married for a short time as a young man. Not long into their marriage his wife had died quite suddenly from a brain tumour. This had devastated him for quite some time but had led him towards a spiritual search that eventually gave him the strength he needed to continue. They all swapped stories into the night and laughed and had fun as if they were all old friends.

In the morning Bill and Sarah arose late and as Bill was making the morning coffee he heard Aaron's voice from the hallway "we've been for a lovely morning walk. It seems we're both morning people, unlike you two lazy bones." Bill turned to see Marion and Aaron grinning at him. They were holding hands.

Bill was startled at first in more ways than one, but after a brief pause he laughed "good to see you two are getting on so well. It might save my bacon for telling Marion about the Junto before I was supposed to."

"Yeah you're a bad lad" Aaron joked "she's definitely on the team."

After breakfast Aaron offered to take Marion back to university. Bill and Sarah stood arm in arm as they waved goodbye to the newfound couple.

Chapter 6 - Psychiatry

"We owe almost all our knowledge not to those who have agreed, but to those who have differed" CC Colton

Bill's research was progressing quite well and he enjoyed his weekly meetings with Tim. Their relationship had developed from mutual respect into a friendship. Their conversations would often digress into more philosophical subjects. Tim had become aware of Bill's discussion group, the science sceptics, but had thus far not come along to any meetings. He explained to Bill that he was reluctant to get involved in anything controversial because he feared losing his job. He had a young family and Bill suspected that he was under some financial pressure.

One morning when Bill went into Tim's office he found him glowing with excitement. "I've been thinking about what you've been saying about evolution Bill. Last night I had some kind of epiphany. I was sitting in the bath daydreaming and thinking about some of the things you've been saying and was looking at my hands when it hit me. I suddenly realised that it just couldn't have come about by chance."

Bill laughed "did you leap up and run down the street naked like Archimedes?"

"No, but I know how he must have felt. Now I'm thinking why couldn't I see it before?"

"I've been told that we only see these things when we are ready" Bill replied. "But the main thing is that you *can* see it. It's quite a breakthrough when you can think outside an existing paradigm that you've been so indoctrinated into."

"Thanks, by the way you have your first progress meeting with Natal this morning."

Bill was slightly apprehensive as he waited for his meeting with Professor Natal. He was glancing through a journal but wasn't really reading. He was distracted by the voice of the young receptionist who was apparently talking to her mother on the phone. The girl was asking about her mother's visit to the doctor.

It seemed from the tone of the conversation and the concern in her voice that her mother must have a terminal illness.

Suddenly Bill was startled by a loud thump and a voice shouting "is that a personal call?" He looked up to see that Professor Natal had come into the room and banged his fist on the table beside the girl's phone. She burst into tears, put down the phone and ran out.

"I've told her before about making personal calls on the university's time" he said in a self satisfied way as he beckoned Bill into his office. "Hopefully that will teach her a lesson."

Bill felt intimidated as Natal glared at him across an enormous desk on which sat a wooden plaque saying "The Boss."

"I'm here to discuss the progress of my thesis" Bill said. "It's just the introduction and outline of my plan at this stage. Did Tim give you a copy?"

"Yes" Natal said as he glossed his eyes over the document in front of him, "any problems?"

"No, not really, Tim has been very helpful" Bill responded.

"Right then it all looks OK. I'm a bit preoccupied at the moment" Natal continued. "I have a faculty meeting to run after this. You'd better come along too. All the staff and postgraduate students are expected to attend."

With that Natal stood up and showed Bill the door. The receptionist looked up and smiled apologetically as Bill walked past, her eyes still glistening and red. "The faculty meeting is in five minutes in the tea room" she stammered.

The small group of staff and graduate students had been gathered in the tearoom for about fifteen minutes before Professor Natal entered causing an eerie hush to fall on the room. It was unusual to see the Professor in the tearoom at all and his presence seemed to create an uncomfortable atmosphere in what was usually a relaxing setting.

The Professor commenced by welcoming some of the new students including Bill and then proceeded to give one of the most self-important and conceited speeches Bill had ever heard. He told about how he had built the faculty into what it was today, he listed his many accomplishments and discoveries including one that Bill knew for a fact was the work done by Tim for his PhD. As Bill was musing on what could make a man so vain and arrogant the speech turned really ugly.

He started to publicly humiliate one of Tim's young postgraduate students. He said the student had put together some shoddy work, was guilty of plagiarism and was unlikely to ever complete his PhD at this university, despite having spent the last three years on it. Natal explained that he was telling the other students about this because he wanted it to be a lesson to the others that he did not accept substandard work. The student in question was forced to listen to the tirade and Bill was amazed that he did not appear to show any emotion.

After the embarrassing meeting Bill followed Tim back to his office.

"What's with that guy?" Bill demanded as soon as they were out of earshot. "Was there any substance to what he was saying about Rick?"

"Not really, it's been more of a personal problem between Natal and Rick. I think Rick's done some good work and the plagiarism accusation is nonsense. The real problem is that Rick has included some findings in his work that contradict the results of the work Natal did in his own thesis years ago. The trouble is Natal doesn't want to hear about it and what's worse is that Natal has spent the last twenty years elaborating and boasting about his original research."

"I see, the poor guy" Bill sighed. "Isn't there anything we can do?"

"I've asked Rick to tone down the conclusions from his study, which he has done but that's not good enough for Natal, who is basically asking Rick to falsify his results. He's a major control freak you know."

"Tell me about it. But surely if he's asking Rick to falsify results, you can take it to higher authorities."

"It's not that simple" Tim complained. "It's only by hearsay via Rick that I know this, there's nothing in writing. It's the word of a student against a long serving Professor. If I take it up with the establishment who's side do you think they'll be on? Even if they believe us they'd be unlikely to do anything about it. They don't like people that rock the boat in the bureaucracy you know. I'd like to take it further myself but I'm between a rock and a hard place. I have my job and my family to think about too."

There was an uncomfortable silence before Bill responded "but what about your self respect, how will you live with yourself?"

"I'll give it some thought, there must be a way" Tim replied. "I thought you'd convinced me there is a God, but if there is how can bastards like Natal continue to get away with this kind of thing?"

"They don't" Bill replied quietly but firmly. "Karma is universal justice and it can't be avoided. It all gets balanced out in the end."

"I hope you're right" Tim replied as Bill got up to leave.

Tim caught up with Bill later that day and said that he would report Natal after all.

Bill praised him and patted him on the back. "It will be for the best" he said kindly.

It was quite late before Bill was able to leave the faculty that day. It was dark as he locked the door behind him. He was surprised to hear a car engine running in the staff car park as he thought everyone was long gone. He looked out into the gloom and could make out a car parked in the Professor's personal parking space but it was not the Professor's car.

"God help me" he shouted as he approached the vehicle. There was a piece of black polythene pipe running from the exhaust pipe and looped back into the window of the car.

"What the hell are you doing" he yelled as he opened the driver's door. Rick's limp body slumped into his arms.

Bill switched the engine off and laid Rick on his back, racking his brains to remember his first aid training. He dialled 000 with one hand while he tried to feel a pulse in Rick's neck with the other. "Thank God" he muttered as he felt a faint pulse. He couldn't feel any breathing though and immediately began expired air resuscitation. He shouted instructions into his mobile phone between breaths pleading with the operator to hurry. He continued the breaths for several minutes before he noticed a slight movement of the chest on its own. He had no idea how long it was before he heard the wailing of the ambulance siren. The efficient ambulance officers took charge and they were soon speeding towards the hospital. Bill was allowed to ride up front after he had pleaded with them to let him come.

At the hospital Rick was taken into emergency and Bill was interviewed by the admissions officer who asked him many questions, most of which he couldn't answer. He barely knew this young man, not even his full name. Not knowing who else to contact, he phoned Tim who was able to obtain next of kin details for the hospital.

Bill waited and was soon joined by Tim who was clearly shaken. "Is he going to be OK?" he asked Bill as he sat next to him.

"I'm sure he'll be OK" Bill responded hesitantly, "he was breathing quite normally when the ambos got there. Does he have any local relatives?"

"Not that I know of, his parents are overseas I believe."

They waited without saying much for some time before a young doctor eventually came into the waiting room to see them. "He's OK" the doctor said "but we've sedated him and would like him to get some rest and we'll get him on some medication. Can you please come back tomorrow morning at visiting time?"

The next morning Bill arose early and drove straight to the hospital. The receptionist was reluctant to let him visit because it wasn't yet official visiting hours but after checking with one of the doctors he was allowed to go in. "The doctor would like to talk to you please before you go" she said as she directed him to the psychiatric ward.

Rick was propped up in bed and he looked like he had a lot more colour in his cheeks than when Bill had last seen him. "They tell me you saved my life" he said managing a sheepish grin, "I'm not sure whether to thank you or curse you. But thanks anyway."

"You gave me quite a shock" Bill replied. "What on earth possessed you to do such a thing?"

"It's complicated" Rick mumbled, looking down, obviously not wanting to meet Bill's eyes. "I've been depressed for a while. I just felt so trapped and it was like there was no way out. I'd invested everything into that project."

"But that's a very permanent solution to a very temporary problem. When you think back, can you think of any problems you've had before that seemed really tough at the time?" Bill asked.

"Well I did have this major crush on a girl when I was a teenager. I guess I thought that was overwhelming at the time when she lost interest in me."

"And is that a problem now?" Bill continued.

"I guess not."

"So that proves these problems are just temporary and as time goes by you will look back on them and think how they were really pretty insignificant. Do you believe in God?"

"I guess so, I'm not sure, my parents are Catholic but I've lost touch with that lately."

"Well if there is a God don't you think He'd be pretty brassed off when He found you'd topped yourself? How would you feel if someone destroyed your beautiful creation? Look maybe I sound like a preacher but I believe the problems we face in life are a gift from God that when we learn to deal with them we grow as human beings. We don't just chuck in the towel when the going gets tough. If things get overwhelming we just need to pray for help and it will come.

And what about your Mum and Dad?" Bill continued. "How would they feel if you'd succeeded in doing yourself in? They've brought you into the world, raised you and this is how you repay them? Look Rick I'm sorry to sound tough but you need to think about this stuff."

Rick sighed "yeah thanks for the lecture and sorry about all that I've put you through."

"You're welcome. I'm just glad I didn't get there five minutes later. And don't worry about your thesis, it will be OK. I have great faith in Tim and I know he will sort it out. I have to go now but I'll come and see you again tomorrow."

Bill then went to his appointment with the young psychiatrist who had a very polite and pleasant manner. He introduced himself as Barry saying he would like to ask Bill a few questions about Rick.

"I don't know how much I can help, I barely know him" Bill declared. "I gave him a bit of a pep talk though about trying to kill himself. He gave me quite a scare."

"That's probably a good thing" Barry replied. "He needs to have the possible consequences of his actions spelled out to him. I hope you weren't too tough on him?"

Bill shook his head "when I imagine how I would feel if it was my son trying to commit suicide I wonder if I was tough enough. What kind of treatment will you be giving him?"

"Just the usual; antidepressants and psychotherapy" Barry replied.

"Not that Freudian nonsense I hope" Bill said disapprovingly.

Barry laughed "so you don't think much of Freud then?"

"No offense, but I'm not a great fan of your whole profession."

"Why is that?" Barry enquired raising his eyebrows.

"It's the way your profession views people, like we are just advanced rats and are solely the product of our environment and our genes. It doesn't acknowledge the human spirit that has free will."

"That's interesting" Barry acknowledged. "Actually I'm not much into Freud either and I certainly don't think people are advanced rats. You might be surprised to know there has been some progress in my profession lately. Nowadays we do try to incorporate a person's spirituality into their treatment because it's been found to work. In fact I was going to ask if you know if Rick has a religion."

"He told me his parents are Catholic" Bill replied. "But I don't think he practices it."

"OK we'll take it up with him. Of course we don't impose religion on anyone or even get involved in it ourselves. We leave that up to the Ministers of the appropriate Church."

Bill nodded "I'm glad you bring faith into the equation because I think that the lack of faith is the main cause of the modern epidemic of depression, anxiety and despair."

"You could be right there, but many people have lost their faith because it's been undermined and discredited by science."

"Tell me about it" Bill agreed.

"Getting back to your point about free will, we do use that concept in cognitive therapy. Have you heard of that?"

"Yes I've read the book "Feeling Good, the New Mood Therapy" by David Burns that describes it pretty well. He explains how negative thinking can be a downward spiral, but that people can be taught to think more positively and thereby avoid depression."

"Exactly, but the challenge for us as practitioners is to convince people they can change their thoughts."

"I don't see how you can when you're coming from the materialist position that your whole profession is based on."

"I'm not a materialist myself" Barry replied "but I know what you mean. I guess you're getting at the neuroscience field."

"Yes, I get really annoyed with the likes of Susan Greenfield who goes around preaching that humans behave according to their involuntary brain function" Bill growled. "I've seen studies in the media where they compare the brain activity of say a depressed person against a "normal" person. They see different activity and conclude that it's the brain activity that causes the behaviour. But if we accept the concept of free will, we would say that the brain activity was caused by our choice. We create the brain activity from the thoughts that we choose.

I saw another study where they interviewed and brain scanned a serial killer. They found little or no activity in his frontal lobe and concluded that he had a genetic defect which manifested in a lack of activity in this "conscience" zone of the brain and that predisposed him to his murderous activities. The murderer of course was delighted because he felt absolved of responsibility for his heinous crimes. But why can't it be that he *chose* not to use this "conscience" function of the brain and that's the reason for the lack of activity in this region."

"You're preaching to the converted here. I *agree* with you" Barry replied. "We can certainly alter our brain and body chemistry from our choice of thoughts. Sex is a prime example.

What a depraved world it would be if we didn't restrain our sexual urges through self control."

Bill chuckled "sorry I do get a bit carried away with myself and I'm not used to anyone agreeing with me. I'm glad to see that Rick's in such good hands."

"That's OK I've enjoyed the chat" Barry replied cheerfully. "So what else can you tell me about Rick?"

Bill explained the problems Rick was having with the university as best he could and that his supervisor was trying to sort it out.

As Bill got up to leave he noticed a putter in the corner of Barry's office. "You're a golfer?" he asked.

"I try" Barry replied, "I'm a bit of a duffer though."

"Same here, maybe we could go out for a hit sometime and continue this conversation" Bill suggested.

"Sure, give me a call" he said giving Bill his business card as he left.

Bill continued to visit Rick in hospital for the two weeks he remained there. In the meantime his parents had returned from overseas and they took Rick back under their wing. Tim arranged for a six month leave of absence for Rick and reassured him that it would all be sorted out when he got back and not to worry about anything.

The complaint that Rick had raised with the university against Professor Natal was not going very well until one day Bill came in to see several policemen escorting him from the building in handcuffs.

"What's going on?" he whispered to Natal's receptionist.

She shrugged her shoulders. "They just came in and arrested him. They took his computer and some CDs as well" she said trying to hide the delight in her voice. "Sorry I shouldn't really be rejoicing."

Bill winked at her and said "I understand."

All was explained in a story that came out in the newspaper the next day that Professor Natal had been arrested for paedophilia. He had been accused of enticing a young boy into bed with him during a recent vacation as well as having child pornography on his computer.

Bill didn't waste any time following up with Barry on his invitation to play golf. Each agreed to bring a partner to make up a foursome.

There were friendly handshakes all round as they queued up to tee off. "This is my friend Dave, he's an intern at the hospital starting his first year of medicine" Barry announced. "He's just a beginner at golf."

Bill introduced Aaron to them "he's a pretty good golfer, single figure handicap. So it might be best if he teamed up with Dave and I play with you Barry."

Aaron teed off first and sent his drive a full three hundred metres down the fairway. "Misspent youth" Aaron explained as the others clapped in awe. Then it was Dave's turn.

His first swing missed the ball by a full six inches. He then followed with two more wild air-shots in quick succession before finally managing to thump the ball about twenty meters from the tee. Bill avoided eye contact with Barry and Aaron as he teed up because he could see they were both struggling to suppress their laughter.

"Relax and don't try to hit it so hard" Aaron suggested as Dave lined up his next shot. Thankfully he made a reasonable fist of the next hit and they were able to set off. As they walked towards the green Barry confided to Bill that Dave was a devoted Christian. He was a mild mannered chap and he warned Bill that they might have to mind their language so as not to offend him.

They made their way through the first few holes with Aaron proving hard to beat even with the large number of shots he was giving to Barry and Bill. Dave continued to duff his way along amidst increasing frustration. At one point he found himself in the bunker. He looked the epitome of concentration as he lined up his shot following Aaron's advice to aim behind the ball. He swung and an enormous amount of sand erupted from the bunker and his ball dropped neatly back into the hole he'd made. It then became a mad frenzy of hacking and shouting at the sand until the ball finally emerged sailing into the bunker on the opposite side of the green. At this he calmly said "right!" walked up to a nearby tree and whacked his sand iron right into the trunk which bent it neatly at right angles.

"That's it; give it a bloody good hiding!" Barry called. "Funny how we play this game to relax" he chortled quietly to Bill who by this time could not hold back his laughter.

Dave ignored the banter as he flung his broken club into a nearby water hazard whilst shouting a tirade of the most disgusting language Bill had heard in a long time. For a moment Dave looked like he was going to cry then he suddenly noticed the others who by this time were all in stitches. His face slowly changed from screwed up anger into a broad grin and he too was soon doubled up with laughter.

"You guys sure know how to entertain a fella" Aaron chuckled as he wiped the tears of laughter from his eyes. He went over and put his hand on Dave's shoulder and said "you'll be right now mate; you just needed to get that out of your system."

Aaron's comment turned out to be prophetic as Dave was now relaxed and as he started to follow Aaron's expert advice he began to hit some quite good shots and even managed to win several holes which enabled an easy win to he and Aaron in the end. At the conclusion of the game they gathered in the clubhouse for a beer and a whiskey or two which was considered the penalty for Dave's air-shots.

The conversation soon turned to medicine. Dave described how he was inspired by his Christian upbringing to become a doctor. This lead into a discussion about what motivates people to do what they do.

"I'm very interested in this topic" Barry said. "One of the biggest problems we have in our profession is with our patients' motivation. We can teach them they *can* think more positively, but if they don't want to do it what can we do?"

"Not very much actually" Aaron chipped in. "People make their own choices and you can't help people that don't want to be helped. Motivation has to come from within a person. Although we do have a role to play in motivating children before bad thinking habits take a foothold. My outdoor centre helps some young people with their motivation by showing them the joy and sense of satisfaction that comes from personal achievement, but very few break the mould set by their parents."

"What about adults though?" Barry asked "is there nothing we can do?"

Aaron looked thoughtful. "We can remind people of the motivation they already have by asking the right questions. But motivation is a very personal thing and each individual is different."

"What do you think about Maslow's hierarchy of needs" Barry asked, "are you familiar with that?"

"Certainly" Aaron replied. "Maslow's hierarchy is a reasonable way of categorising people's motivations. The main problem I have with it is the assumption that people naturally progress up the pyramid as each need is met. If people were just animals with built in instincts it might work like this, but we're not. We all have free will to choose.

Even at the lowest level on the hierarchy where survival is paramount people still have choices. For example the soldier who threw himself on a grenade to save his friends gave up his very survival for the higher cause of saving his friends. Another example is after a natural disaster where a person who has lost everything chips in and helps his neighbour to rebuild.

At the other end of the scale there are quite self-fulfilled people that are still motivated by such base animal desires as lust, jealously or revenge. Also at the top of the scale there are people that have as many material possessions as one could possibly want and yet they are still motivated by greed for more.

On the other hand we see people who are born into wealthy families with everything they could possibly need already available to them and yet we see them become high achievers, devoting their lives to the service of others, to charity work and so on. Why do they do it?"

Aaron paused as Barry interrupted "what about social needs, the next level on Maslow's hierarchy? Many in my field say that most of our motivation comes from our being social animals."

"Indeed," Aaron replied "the need to belong or to be loved is for most people the overriding motivation. It starts with peer pressure in children and the need for approval by others remains the dominant force in many people's lives. Our families, ethnic groups, cultures, religions and institutions all rely on this motivation. But that isn't the end of it.

Ego is Maslow's next level. Children have sibling rivalry and competitiveness can continue to dominate our motivation. This can be a mild desire to seek attention and wanting to impress others all the way to the control freaks that want above all else to dominate others. This unfortunately is what motivates most of our political and religious leaders and even the leaders of our social and professional institutions.

Maslow's highest level is self-actualisation and we could compare this to spiritual concepts such as achieving sainthood, enlightenment, or greatness. We could also include freedom in this. But again I maintain that we can be motivated by the higher levels without having met any of the other so-called needs."

"So what do you think motivates people to greatness?" Bill, who had been listening quietly, asked.

"The highest level of motivation is based on love and comes from a position of faith" Aaron responded. "Without faith we are mere animals living a meaningless life seeking to maximise our pleasure and minimise our pain, but with faith and love we're motivated by an inner strength.

I suspect this high level motivation in its purest sense is quite rare. Sometimes we kid ourselves that we're doing something out of love for others. But if we're really honest with ourselves and truly examine our intensions we might find we're doing it out of ego to show others how "good" we are, or perhaps we're just trying to gain acceptance by our chosen group."

"So how do we know that we're not *all* doing so-called good deeds for ulterior motives?" Barry asked.

"Because we have the example of the truly great ones in history, and we see it in our everyday lives. There are many people who are genuinely doing what they believe is right and are working towards the betterment of themselves and their fellow man" Aaron said with finality.

There was quite a long pause before Barry said "so is there anything we can do about motivating others?"

"On a practical level if we are to help people motivate themselves we need to tap into a special interest that they may have. For example if a person has a hobby or sport they will be motivated to pursue something that ties in with it. Also we can encourage people to set goals and start working towards them. The process of setting goals is of itself motivational. Once you have a purpose you're motivated towards it and when we take action towards the goals the motivation increases" Aaron concluded.

The conversation then switched to science and Bill talked about the science sceptics group. "I'm looking for a speaker for next week if anyone's interested" he said.

Dave said that he had an idea for a speech on science and medicine he'd like to do.

After the younger men left Aaron remained to discuss progress with Bill. "You might have two good contenders right there" he said. "They're both very impressive; we might be able to start putting this thing together very soon. We need to help Dave through that anger problem though."

Aaron said he would stay over for a few days so that he could listen to Dave's speech but Bill knew he had another motive. He was spending time a lot of time with Marion.

Chapter 7 - Medicine

"Under normal conditions the research scientist is not an innovator but a solver of puzzles, and the puzzles upon which he concentrates are just those which he believes can be both stated and solved within the existing scientific tradition" Thomas Kuhn

There had been increasing interest in the science sceptics and there was a good crowd for Dave who had brought Barry along for moral support. Tim had also finally agreed to come along. He had been promoted to Associate Professor since Natal was gone.

Dave's speech was entitled: *"The limitations of science and modern medicine."*

"Most published research findings are false!" he began boldly, pausing to gauge the effect of his opening statement on the audience. "This is a big claim, but it's a claim made in a published paper in 2005 by John Ioannidis. Could it really be true, that more than half of published scientific findings are wrong? How is this possible?

If it is true, could this be why we've made virtually no scientific discoveries in the last fifty years?" There was a murmuring in the audience. "You don't believe me?" Dave asked. "I put it to you that almost all modern technologies are based on scientific discoveries made more than fifty years ago: penicillin, DNA, radio, television, computers, radar, satellite, even lasers, I could go on.

Ladies and Gentlemen today I'm going to tell you how the modern science system works, why we continue to get the wrong answers and how this inhibits our progress, especially in medicine. First we need to look at how science is done." Dave wrote up on the whiteboard:

1) The scientific paradigm – Thomas Kuhn

"Has anyone heard of Kuhn's scientific paradigm?"

A member of the audience suggested "is that the set of currently accepted concepts and theories held by a group of scientists at any point in time, and scientists of that era don't step outside its bounds?"

"That's exactly right" Dave replied "and that means no thinking outside the paradigm. Or we could say *no creative thinking allowed!*

Scientists only test and interpret results within the current accepted paradigm. Scientists are taught perhaps even indoctrinated into accepting a certain view of their field and most will not even consider anything outside that paradigm. It's like the religious person who has grown up in a certain community that views the world in a particular way. Scientists are no different. For example in my profession the human being is viewed as a piece of live meat that behaves according to its brain which is in turn purely a physiological organ. This organ is merely a complex animal brain that has evolved by chance through random genetic mutations.

There is no acknowledgement in modern medicine of even the possibility of a human spirit or soul with free will and the ability to heal. Illness is viewed as a purely physiological phenomenon. The "diagnosis" of physiological illnesses has rapidly increased. Depression has been labelled a disease. There are all manner of disorders and syndromes, new ones named every year. In children we supposedly have an epidemic of attention deficit disorder which we treat by prescribing drugs that we put adults in jail for taking. Is this epidemic of depression, disorders and syndromes real or are we just obsessed with wanting to diagnose something that we can prescribe a pill to fix? Or maybe a placebo would do?" Dave paused for his audience to consider his rhetorical question.

"The placebo is a really interesting phenomenon. It's an example of professional blindness in action. We doctors will not acknowledge spiritual healing even when it occurs right under our very noses. We believe in the placebo effect so much that we even use it in treating patients. Doctors prescribe antibiotics for the common cold or influenza when they know full well that it does nothing physiologically. There are some estimates that thirty-five to forty percent of all official prescriptions are basically "impure" placebos. This is our medical ritual. Patient goes to doctor; doctor writes prescription, patient goes away with pills satisfied and is probably cured.

In this regard we are no better than the plethora of so-called alternative medicines that have all manner of potions, rituals and hocus-pocus. The result for the patient is mostly to do with how confidently the practitioner expresses their belief in the treatment and how well this faith is conveyed to the patient. Don't misunderstand me I do accept there are real physiological effects of drugs. My point is that the placebo effect is just another name for faith healing.

If we accept that the placebo effect is real we are accepting that faith healing works but we don't have a clue how. We can't even investigate it because it doesn't fit the paradigm where miracles just don't happen."

Dave then wrote up his second argument:

2) The peer review system

He continued "the peer review system is the accepted method under which research results are published and the only peers permitted to review scientific work are those that are deeply entrenched in the prevailing paradigm. These are also the peers who have reached the top of the ego pile and whose powerful positions and reputations are threatened by any challenge to the paradigm itself. Scientists who have spent their careers elaborating particular aspects of a mistaken theory are understandably unwilling to change their view. Who could accept that one's life's work to date is based on a lie?

This problem has been exacerbated today by modern communication and transport systems. Because of the internet and cheap air travel the anonymity of scientific investigation and peer review is gone. Readers are biased when they see the names on the scientific papers because they know who they are. Anyone who is from outside the club is considered a "stirrer" and is immediately written off in the mind of the reviewer. Even a well researched study will not be considered, more than likely not even read, if it is written by someone who is seen to be rocking the boat. Preconceived prejudice overrides reason. This is actually a continuation of what happens in the school yard. The "in crowd" often led by bullies ostracises the non-conformist and for most people the need to belong surpasses the need to think."

Dave again paused to write up his next heading:

3) Motivation for research

"We need to consider where the motivation for any particular scientific study has come from and in particular how it is funded. All studies have an agenda that is usually determined by the funding source. Commercially based research is aimed at increasing the long term profitability of the industry or enterprise providing the funding. Results that don't help this goal will not see the light of day. Even if the link to the funding body is quite remote there is still pressure to find the "right" results to ensure that future funding will be forthcoming.

Research that is motivated by the non-commercial sector on the other hand is usually motivated by a political agenda and is often at odds with commercial interests. Much of this research is driven by groups that have a particular barrow to push about a cause to which they are emotionally attached. This type of research has increased dramatically in recent years where social and environmental concerns have dominated the public arena.

There are a couple of interesting problems going on with this type of research. The first is that it tends to get a disproportionate share of public funding because minority groups that have a strong emotional attachment to the issue push their case forward in emotive language that attracts political attention. Government funds are often forthcoming if it is seen to be politically correct or in a "good cause." For example the green movement has in recent years gained a large share of the public purse by maintaining that the planet and it's fluffy cute Polar Bears are in danger owing to man's activities.

The other problem is when a particular cause is seen to be "good" or virtuous. Advocates can get away with putting forward much less rigorously tested results. In some cases results have been deliberately falsified. This is deemed to be OK because it's "in a good cause." Again the green movement is a prime example where Al Gore and others have deliberately exaggerated and present unsubstantiated and even false evidence to advance their cause about global warming. The false results are further promoted by the media who also wish to be seen on the side which is most politically correct. In the modern day the media has the most profound effect on public opinion, so he who controls the media controls public opinion."

At this point Bill looked across at Jeff who was in the audience and winked. Jeff smiled back as Dave continued.

"There are some Government funded bodies that are supposed to be providing pure and unbiased scientific research. However again this is impossible. Research proposals and funding are always tainted by political concerns and are therefore driven by the need for political gain which is in turn driven by the desire to hang onto power.

There is almost no unbiased scientific research. Even wealthy philanthropists who finance some research have their own personal biases that are based on their view of the world. Perhaps the only remaining unbiased science is being done in a back shed somewhere by an amateur and perhaps eccentric inventor. Or maybe there is someone out there playing around with ideas while working as a patent clerk. That concludes my talk. Are there any questions?" Dave concluded amidst the applause.

A young man asked "you say there's all this bias but even if its true how do we falsify results?"

Dave responded "I mentioned Ioannidis at the beginning of my talk. He cited in his paper poor experimental design, poor interpretation of results and misuse of statistics. It isn't really very hard to falsify results and in many cases we may do it unwittingly or subconsciously. Experiments are set up to prove rather than to disprove the accepted paradigm. Scientists usually find what they expect to find and if anything doesn't fit it's treated as an outlier or ignored.

When we look for other work to support our findings we pick the studies that agree with us and ignore the rest. Sometimes false findings can become entrenched when one study is continually cited if it suits the agenda of the current researcher even if it has been refuted many times over by other studies. This is how scientific dogma becomes an old wives tale. Nobody goes back and checks the original source. We often find this in studies about health food and especially about whether this or that food or product either causes or prevents cancer."

"You mention cancer" said another member of the audience, "do you think we'll ever find a cure?"

"Good question. Cancer research is a good example of what I've been talking about. Despite spending billions of dollars over many decades we've made little progress. In the USA the number of people diagnosed with cancer is nearly double what it was thirty-five years ago. Most of the progress we've made has been from earlier diagnosis.

It's relatively easy to raise money for cancer research because so many people have lost loved ones to it. Therefore it's become a gravy train for the researchers. So we end up with thousands of studies that have found that everything from sliced bread to coffee can cause cancer and thousands that say the opposite.

Do I think we will ever find a cure for cancer? Not when we continue to investigate it within the current paradigm. When we limit ourselves to the materialist view of the body and ignore the human spirit we will not significantly progress our understanding of cancer and many other conditions.

Many doctors now acknowledge that mental processes can dramatically affect a patient's outcomes when they have been diagnosed with cancer. Patients with a positive outlook can significantly increase their life span. There have also been many cases of what we might call miracle cures where patients have recovered for unexplained reasons or sometimes as a result of alternative medical remedies. Why does this happen? We don't know. But the point is conventional medicine is not interested in investigating it because it doesn't accept the possibility that it's true, even when we observe it happening in front of our very noses. We need to investigate these miracle cures with an open mind."

Another question came from the floor "alternative medicines such as homeopathy have been undergoing a folk revival lately. Do you think there is any value in these alternative treatments?"

"I think there is value in some of these treatments but I suspect that the vast majority of them are due to the placebo effect. Most of the scientific studies that have tested alternative treatments find that they have little or no clinical effect over and above the placebo. But of course we have to consider those factors we talked about earlier and that even conventional medicine has a large component of the placebo effect.

Actually I have a gripe with most of these natural remedies. There's a double standard in the system. Pharmaceuticals have to go through a rigorous testing process whereas many of these alternative cures have no testing at all and they are often promoted to the public through the media based on completely unsubstantiated and even false claims. Are there any more questions?"

Barry asked "you talked about various syndromes and disorders being diagnosed. To what extent do you believe that these are psychosomatic?"

"Thanks for the question" Dave grinned. "I actually have a disorder myself known as the crazy angry golfer syndrome as you have observed. Seriously though, I try to avoid the word psychosomatic. We tend to relate this word to hypochondria and there's a perception that psychosomatic illness is not a real illness. And yet symptoms of illness are still there. Whether it's psychosomatic or not the illness is real to the patient.

I believe that much of the illness we have in our modern society is brought on by ourselves through hypochondria and fear. Sometimes when we fear something we can end up getting it. Illness is also brought on in children by overanxious parents due to their fears which may carry right through their children's lives.

Also sickness can be brought on by a desire to appear disabled in some way. For example we may want to be excused from a challenging situation or to have an excuse for our underachievement. I don't think the distinction between psychosomatic and physiological is very clear. We have time for one more question."

Bill posed the final question. "Dave, you've told us some of your reservations with modern medicine but there must also be many positive features in modern medicine?"

"Of course, thanks for bringing that up Bill. I hope I haven't given the impression that I lack confidence in modern medicine. Actually the opposite is true. I am after all myself a medical doctor trained within our wonderful system. It may not be perfect but it's the best that we have. Modern medicine has increased our life expectancy tremendously. We've made huge gains in treating heart disease, chronic illnesses and many kinds of surgery. Our diagnostic systems have also greatly improved so that even cancer can be treated effectively through early diagnosis. My own mother was diagnosed with breast cancer and was able to be treated successfully and she's now in remission. Let's be clear about this, I'm on the side of modern medicine. I just think we need to examine the current paradigm. We need to teach people to take more responsibility for their own health through preventative means and positive thinking. That way they'll be less dependent on the medical profession so that I can have some time to improve my golf game." Dave smiled and said he'd better leave it there.

After the speech Aaron asked Bill to get some people together for coffee. "It's time we started to put this thing together" he said.

And so the first gathering of the Science Junto was held over a cup of coffee although, of the seven people in attendance, only three understood the true significance of the meeting. Aaron explained that he and Bill were getting together a group of open minded and concerned scientists to discuss and monitor the direction of scientific thought. He requested the group remain secret so that they could assess the character and motives of potential new members. He suggested those present give it some thought and they would meet back in a month.

As they went their separate ways Bill turned on his mobile phone and found he had several missed calls from Sarah and there was a message to get in touch with her urgently. "It's about Rosie" Sarah said. "She's in a bad way; we need to go and see her."

Bill knew that Sarah was talking about her younger sister who lived in Sydney. "How bad is she?" Bill asked.

"Pretty bad, she can't even get out of bed. Jody has been looking after her apparently but she's reaching the end of her tether. It was Jody who rang."

"OK I'll be home soon. We'd better go and see her" Bill replied.

After some hurried packing and a long car trip they greeted Rosie's daughter Jody outside the house. "I can't get her to see a doctor" Jody said. "She's so stubborn, but I can't cope any more." As they went in they noticed pill bottles lying around everywhere containing various homeopathic remedies. Rosie was a trained nurse but had become obsessed with homeopathic medicine and naturopathy in recent years.

It was a sad sight as they entered into Rosie's bedroom. The curtains were closed and she was just lying there in the dim light. "Sorry I can't get up and get you a cup of tea" she groaned. "It's my back, it's nothing much, I just need to get some bed rest."

After the initial greetings Jody took them aside and confessed that Rosie had been this way for months. Jody had been feeding her and catering for her every need. "This is ridiculous" Sarah said, "call an ambulance Bill."

The ambulance arrived and Rosie kicked up a huge fuss and refused to budge. Sarah shouted at her sister "you're damned well going to the hospital whether you like it or not! You can't carry on doing this to your daughter!"

After much shouting and protesting they eventually managed to load Rosie into the ambulance. When she eventually reached the hospital she had calmed down somewhat and now appeared to be resigned to her fate.

"We'll keep her in for observation and the doctor will do some tests" said the sympathetic nurse as they helped Rosie into a hospital bed.

They waited anxiously with Jody for the next few days while Rosie had her tests and they visited her daily. She had cheered up considerably and now seemed to enjoy being waited on by the nurses. "It's quite good to be on the receiving end for a change" she chuckled.

One day when they went in to visit her, the doctor called them into a consulting room and said "its bad news I'm afraid, she's probably only got a few weeks to live." There was a stunned silence followed by a loud sob from Jody. Sarah wrapped her arms around her young niece as she wept uncontrollably.

"Isn't there anything you can do doctor?" Bill asked.

"I'm afraid not. She's way too far gone to operate. It probably started in her breast some time ago, perhaps even years, but now it's got into her bones and unfortunately there's nothing we can do. If only she had come to see us earlier" he sighed.

Rosie only lived for three weeks after being admitted to hospital.

Chapter 8 - Geology

"A new scientific truth does not triumph by convincing its opponents and making them see the light, but rather because its opponents eventually die, and a new generation grows up that is familiar with it" Max Planck

Bill and Sarah arrived home from Rosie's funeral exhausted after helping Jody with arrangements. They invited Jody to stay with Sarah for a few weeks while she got her life back together. On arriving home, there was a message on the answer phone from an old friend of Bill's from his younger days at university. Nigel had moved to Queensland after a long period overseas and wanted to meet up with Bill for a beer.

Bill was keen to catch up with Nigel, not just because they were old mates, but also because Nigel was a geologist and Bill had long wanted to discuss some ideas with him about the geology of the earth that had intrigued him since he had lived in volcanically active New Zealand.

It was twenty-five years since Bill had seen Nigel and he had changed a lot from the scruffy long haired bearded young man he used to know. He was now a very well dressed clean cut businessman.

"You haven't changed a bit" Bill grinned as they shook hands.

"Thanks, well I don't feel any different, but I try not to look in the mirror" Nigel joked. "You're quite well preserved yourself."

They exchanged brief life stories since they had parted ways all those years ago. Nigel had a family that was now grown up and he had recently divorced from his wife. He had spent most of his life working for a big oil company that had moved him around the world to various exotic locations. His job didn't make for a good family life but he had enjoyed his work and was passionate about the oil industry.

"So where are we with oil?" Bill asked. "Are we going to run out of it soon?"

"Very hard to say" Nigel shook his head. "Judging from the prices you'd think so, but we really don't know how much oil we have left. Much of what's left is under countries that don't necessarily tell us the truth and they keep changing their stories. Iran, Iraq, Saudi Arabia, Venezuela and Russia are difficult countries to deal with at the best of times and unfortunately they are going to increasingly hold us to ransom over oil. We're still finding more oil but its getting harder to fight against the greenies who think a couple of seals are worth more than the whole future prosperity of mankind. Then on the demand side you've got China soaking it up like there's no tomorrow. It sure is getting grim."

"What can we do to fix it then?" Bill asked. "I'm interested because I'm in agriculture and I'm concerned to see good agricultural land and resources now going into bio-fuel production when we're still trying to feed a hungry world."

"I have thought about this a lot" Nigel replied. "I agree with you that bio-fuels aren't the answer. It's a problem that needs a multipronged approach. First of all we need to cut wasted consumption. For instance here in Australia having all these trucks driving one after the other between capital cities is ridiculous. We need to fix the rail system. Trains are far more efficient."

"And that would reduce our road accidents involving trucks too" Bill agreed.

"Sure would. Secondly we need to look into our transport systems in the major cities. In some cases improving public transport will help, but let's face it most people don't want to give up their independence. So I reckon we need to substitute our petrol and diesel powered vehicles for either hydrogen or electric hybrids within major city limits. That would cut petrol consumption dramatically. We can't drive fast in cities anyway and when people drive outside city limits they can switch back to petrol. We'll solve city air pollution at the same time."

Bill nodded "what about the electricity and the hydrogen though, won't that be costly?"

"Well there's a problem with the cost of hydrogen production at the moment" Nigel admitted, "but when we solve that it will be a good option. It's the most clean burning fuel there is. In the meantime electricity is no problem. We've already got a good distribution system set up for that and we've got plenty of coal to keep us going."

Bill grinned "so you're not a CO_2 fascist then?"

"Hell no!" Nigel laughed. "Bring on the CO_2. Doesn't it make our plants grow faster?"

"Sure does" Bill chuckled as Nigel got up to buy another round of beer. When he returned Bill said "there's something I'd like to ask your opinion about."

"Fire away."

"Well it concerns the ice ages and what causes them" Bill started.

"There have been quite a few theories about the ice ages" Nigel interrupted. "I think the most popular theory these days has something to do with the path of the earth around the sun, but it doesn't really match up with the irregularity of the ice ages."

"Yes" Bill nodded, "but have you heard about the Earth crust displacement theory?"

"No, tell me about it."

"Well the theory is that the entire crust of the earth periodically shifts around its liquid interior mantel. So the ice that's previously built up at the old poles will melt because it's moved to warmer latitudes. At the same time ice will reform at the new poles. If the theory is right the Hudson Bay was at the North Pole during what we call the last ice age. This would explain why most of the North American continent and North Western Europe were covered in ice during the last ice age, while Alaska and Siberia on the other side were relatively ice free. There were many species of mega fauna such as Mammoths, Woolly Rhinoceroses and Sabre Tooth Tigers living in Northern Siberia and Alaska during the last ice age where nothing can survive today because of the cold. They all became extinct at the end of the ice age."

"So you're saying that the earth wasn't actually colder during the last ice age" Nigel pondered. "It's just that different parts of the surface were in the cold region."

"Precisely" Bill answered.

"What is the proposed cause of the shift?" Nigel asked with increasing interest.

"It's to do with the distribution of ice near the poles. When there's a continental land mass near a pole, ice will build up on that land mass according to its shape. Because the continent is unlikely to be exactly symmetrical on the pole, the weight of the ice build up will also be unevenly distributed. As this imbalance increases there becomes a critical point where centrifugal force causes the whole crust of the earth to slip around so that the heavy bit moves towards the equator. A good analogy is when you put too many clothes in one side of the washing machine."

"Yeah I've been there!" Nigel exclaimed. "Bloody washing machine made a horrendous crashing noise and started jumping across the floor. But go on. This sounds intriguing, who thought this theory up?"

"Hugh Brown came up with the theory about the ice imbalance in the 1940s, but he believed that the whole planet may have periodically shifted on its axis. The pole shift theory itself seems to be older. Charles Darwin's son George also apparently speculated about a shift in the planet's rotation.

Brown was an engineer and he knew the importance of having a flywheel centred absolutely precisely. He came up with the idea that if an icecap built up off-centre at one of the poles it would create a centrifugal force, which would tend to throw the heavy side of the pole towards the equator.

Anyway, in the 1950s along came Charles Hapgood, a science historian who was attracted to the theory. He asked his friend and co-writer Campbell to test Brown's theory. Campbell concluded from formulae used for calculating centrifugal force, that Brown's scenario was impossible. The force created by an off-centre icecap could not cause a shift in the pole proposed by Brown. This is because the earth has a bulge around the equator that helps to stabilise the spin like a gyroscope. So this rotational stability is much greater than any destabilising influence at the poles.

Then apparently Campbell suggested that there might be enough force to displace the crust over its underlying layers assuming that there is a liquid mantel under the crust. Hapgood was hooked and spent much of the rest of his life investigating and writing about the theory. He wasn't alone; he had support from Albert Einstein, no less, who wrote the foreword to one of Hapgood's books."

"It all sounds very plausible but why do you think this theory was abandoned?" Nigel queried.

"Well I guess it's like a lot of scientific theories that come and go. You must have learned at Uni about Lyell's uniformitarian theories that all geological change is slow."

Nigel nodded "yes, Lyell was one of the fathers of modern geological theory."

"Well" Bill continued "because the crust displacement process apparently happens relatively quickly it was considered to be catastrophism which didn't fit the uniformitarian model. Also the fact that Hapgood was a science historian rather than a geologist meant he was easily discredited.

The other reason I think the theory was rejected by mainstream geology is that Hapgood's theory coincided with the development of the continental drift theory and plate tectonics, which has become widely accepted. But I think continental drift and earth crust displacement could both be happening. One doesn't rule out the other. There was a Chinese researcher, Ma, who proposed there were two separate mechanisms at work, based on a lifetime of study of coral formations."

"How long is the displacement process supposed to take?" Nigel asked.

"Hapgood theorised that it could be over several hundred years but it could be much quicker than that, who knows? There's some ice core data around these days that shows rapid climate change in only a few years."

"Yes I've heard about that" Nigel agreed, "but even if it was hundreds of years that's like the batting of an eyelid in geological terms."

"So, from what I've told you, do you think it's possible?" Bill asked finally.

"Maybe" Nigel responded. "It's funny you should mention this. I was just reading in a journal the other day about some work that was being done by some Norwegians that proved the earth's crust has done exactly what you've been talking about in the past. Something about mantel dynamics they called it if I remember rightly."

"That's interesting" Bill replied "because Einstein's only doubt about the theory was whether the earth's crust can be moved easily enough over the inner layers. And you say that it may now have been proved that this has indeed happened."

Nigel interrupted "yes but they were talking about something that happened over a much longer time frame. I think they were talking about millions of years."

"But if it can happen over a long time frame why not a short one?" Bill asked.

"Perhaps" Nigel conceded, "and as you say there's been some interesting results from ice core data from Greenland and Antarctica. Is there any indication when the next crust displacement will occur?"

"Not really" Bill responded "there's no way we can calculate when it will happen again because we don't know what's going on down at the level of the mantel. But the likelihood of it happening is increasing all the time."

Bill pulled a small globe from his bag, held it upside down and pointed to Antarctica. "This is where it's all happening now" he said. "The Antarctic ice cap is enormous and several kilometres thick. But see how the bulk of the ice is on the eastern side of the pole. In fact ninety percent of the world's ice is contained there and it's continuing to thicken all the time. On the other side there's comparatively little ice as it's mostly sea and the Western Antarctic peninsular is actually melting quite rapidly. This is the area the greenies are referring to when they talk about melting ice in Antarctica. This rapid melting is accelerating the imbalance."

"So the greenies might have something to worry about after all from the melting ice" Nigel chuckled. "OK, we don't know when it will go, but I assume we do know which way it will go because that Eastern Antarctic sheet will push towards the equator."

"Exactly" Bill replied "and we can also estimate how far it might go too. Hapgood and Campbell calculated that the centre of gravity of the ice cap on Antarctica is about 500 to 550 kilometres from the South Pole."

"This is all quite fascinating!" Nigel exclaimed. "I'm actually taking some long service leave at the moment so I'd like to investigate this a bit more. Have you got some literature on this, books and so on?"

"Lots" Bill smiled.

Chapter 9 - Astronomy

"Most cosmologists have spent all of their careers, or at least the past twenty-five years elaborating various aspects of the Big Bang. It would be very difficult for them, as for any scientist, to abandon their life's work" Eric J Lerner

It was a week later when Nigel met up again with Bill. "I've been studying this Earth crust displacement theory and I still don't know if it's true" he said, "but if it is it would play havoc with our civilisation next time it happens."

"It sure would" Bill agreed. "On the plus side man has survived these things before but, as you say, it would most likely destroy our civilisation. The thing is though we haven't a clue when it might happen. It might be in a thousand years, ten thousand years or next week. So there's not much point in worrying about it. Did you find any more evidence that might make you either believe or reject the theory?"

"Not really" Nigel replied. "I tried to discuss the theories with some of my geologist colleagues but they weren't in the least bit interested. I found it surprising they wouldn't even get into a discussion about it. They told me not to delve into crackpot theories. But if Einstein was a crackpot then call me a crackpot.

One interesting thing I did find was that there are many soothsayers, doomsday cults and religious groups out there that have hooked into Hapgood's theories. There was one group that believed there would be an Earth crust displacement in the year 2000 because of a planetary alignment scenario. The poor saps must be still waiting I guess. What do you make of all that?"

"I have to admit that I was sucked into some of that millennium stuff myself in the 1990s" Bill said sheepishly. "It might sound silly to you now but the way I understood it then it was quite feasible. The prediction was that the earth is ready for a crust displacement and when all the planets lined up with the sun and the moon the additional gravitational pull would be enough to trigger the displacement.

After some research though I decided that the planetary alignment scenario would be unlikely to trigger anything because the gravitational force from the planets is minute compared to the moon and the sun and therefore irrelevant. I'm still taken by the idea that tidal forces could trigger the displacement though. I know for a fact that tidal forces can trigger volcanic eruptions."

"How do you know that tidal forces cause eruptions?" Nigel asked with surprise.

"I didn't say cause; I said trigger, in the way that a mouse can trigger an avalanche if it's ready to go. I've observed it. I used to live within sight of several volcanoes in New Zealand. I noticed that when Ruapehu was erupting repeatedly at one stage it would blow its top regularly on the new moon. The new moon's when the sun lines up with the moon which adds about an additional forty percent to the normal tidal pull of the moon. When you think about it it's quite logical. The moon shifts our tides to and fro twice a day. Magma is also liquid so why wouldn't it be affected the same way?"

"I suppose so" Nigel nodded. "So do you think tidal forces might be a significant factor in volcanic eruptions?"

"Almost certainly" Bill replied. "I checked the dates of the major volcanic eruptions of the twentieth century and found that many of them were at a new moon perigee including Mount Pelée, Mount Pinatubo and Nevado del Ruiz. Even the recent eruption of the Columbian volcano Nevado del Huila that hadn't erupted for five hundred years was right on cue. While Mount St Helens didn't have its major eruption on a new moon perigee, it actually began its eruptions a couple of months before on one."

"Remind me what perigee means" Nigel interrupted.

"Perigee is when the moon is at its closest monthly approach to the earth on its elliptical path. Because the earth is also going around the sun there's a difference between the perigee cycle and the new moon cycle. There are about twenty-seven and a half days between perigees and about twenty-nine and a half between new moons. Consequently about every fourteen months there's a concurrence between the perigee and the new moon. That's when we get spring tides or king tides as they call them in Australia."

"That's amazing Bill, why hasn't anyone else noticed this relationship?"

"Well perhaps some have, but volcanologists spend all their time looking down and astronomers look up and they don't talk to each other much."

"What about earthquakes, did you find any relationship there?"

"Good question" Bill replied. "I suspect that some types of earthquakes may be triggered by tidal forces but I couldn't find a good correlation. I think earthquakes are more complicated."

"This perigee new moon thing interests me" Nigel mused. "If the moon and the sun were at maximum pulling power maybe an additional line up of planets could make a difference, what do you reckon?"

Bill shook his head "I'm sceptical about the effect of the planets these days."

"My mate Pete is an astronomer maybe we could run it past him. He works at an observatory out west. I can send him an email."

"Sure why not" Bill agreed.

Several days later Bill received a copy of an email reply from Nigel's friend Pete that read as follows:

Dear Nigel

Thank you for your interesting email. You've asked me about the tidal affects of the moon, the sun and our main planets. Firstly you are right in your assessment that the tidal affect of our planets is very small in comparison with the moon. Tidal force is proportional to the mass and inversely proportional to the cube of the distance. So a change in distance affects the force much more than does a change in mass. This is why the moon has the major affect on our tides. However the sun still has quite a big affect even though it's a long way away because of its massive size.

The planets do nevertheless have some tidal affect which I will endeavour to calculate for you. There are only three planets worth calculating: Venus, because it is quite close to us when it is on our side of the sun, and Jupiter and Saturn because they are so large. Jupiter's mass actually accounts for about 70% of the total mass of all the planets combined and Saturn is a further 20%. You have said that you are only interested in alignments where tidal forces come from the same direction therefore we can safely ignore Mars which would be on the other side of the sun in your alignment scenario.

So if we consider an alignment that would provide the maximum "pull" on the earth from one direction we would have an alignment of Saturn, Jupiter, Sun, Venus, Moon and Earth. I have calculated that Venus would contribute an affect approximately equal to the moon being about six kilometres closer to the Earth. The next in line is Jupiter which would contribute the same tidal force as the moon being about 200 metres closer to the Earth. The affect of Saturn is about 10 meters.

You might not be familiar with the complicated path the moon makes in its orbit around the Earth. While there is a perigee once every twenty seven days or so, the moon at perigee is not always the same "closeness" to the Earth. It varies according to an eighteen year cycle. Some perigees are as close as about 356,500 km whereas others are as far away as 370,000 km. Therefore in the scheme of things you might as well forget about the planets.

So if you are looking for maximum tidal forces you need to know the distance of the moon from the Earth at perigee. Maximum tidal force will occur when the new moon coincides with a "close" perigee. I am sending you some calendars that show perigee distances and dates for the next 50 years along with dates for new moon.

The other thing you might want to consider is the timing and "exactness" of the alignments. The moon and the sun do not always coincide exactly each month at new moon. When they do of course we get a solar eclipse. Also there will normally be a time difference between the perigee and the new moon. Sometimes the two events will occur very closely, say within one hour, whereas at other times they may occur up to six or seven hours apart.

This has been an interesting exercise. Do you think I should avoid visiting volcanic regions when the new moon coincides with perigee? Why don't you come and pay me a visit at the observatory one day. There are some stunning images I can show you through the telescope and we can discuss this further.

Regards

Pete

Soon after receiving this email Nigel phoned Bill to announce he had decided to take Pete up on his offer and go and visit him. Bill was quite pleased because Nigel had been distracting him from his study lately.

Bill's research was progressing steadily aided by Tim who was very supportive. Since his promotion he was in very good spirits and the mood of the entire faculty was happier since the departure of Natal. There appeared to be little chance of his returning because he had pleaded guilty to the sex offences and was now in jail. Rick had come back early to complete his thesis and now appeared to be motivated and contented.

Bill continued to run the tutorial for Hillary's organic class and to do her marking. His relationship with her had not improved and he now barely had any contact with her. One day she did not come in for her class and Bill was asked to fill in for her. It turned out she had been admitted to a mental institution and was unlikely to be back for some time. Bill was asked to tidy up her outstanding paper work as best he could. When he went through her files he was appalled to find dozens of unmarked assignments dating back years.

The month since Dave's speech had gone by quickly and the seven potential members of the Science Junto met on schedule. Bill explained to the new group that he and Aaron had conceived of the idea of the Science Junto based on Benjamin Franklin's model. A modified version of the Junto creed was agreed upon and the seven members were sworn in. Bill decided at the same time to subtly wind up the science sceptics group as it had largely achieved its purpose in bringing together the new group.

A few days later Bill and Aaron attended a primary Junto meeting. Bill presented a report on the successful inauguration of the Science Junto and explained that he was hopeful of completing the membership base before long. He explained that he believed the matter of highest priority for the Junto was climate change alarmism. He gave a précis of Jeff's speech and explained that the Australian government was soon likely to follow other western countries in wasting billions of taxpayer dollars on the futile process of cutting carbon emissions.

He received a warm round of applause and congratulations on his progress. The group agreed with his assessment of the climate change scenario. Hamish suggested that Jeff could be very useful if he was able to infiltrate the environmental hierarchy in order to assess vulnerabilities and to work out methods of attack. In the meantime members of both Juntos would be encouraged to talk up the truth about climate change wherever possible and to work with other sceptics to disseminate facts that would discredit the climate change alarmists.

Aaron and Bill subsequently met with Jeff to ask him to "play the game" so he could penetrate the environmental movement. Aaron emphasised the importance of Jeff's mission and that it was an extremely worthy project that would greatly benefit his country and mankind.

Jeff was delighted with the prospect of being a spy for the Science Junto. "At last I'll feel like I'm doing something useful" he said. "It'll be quite exciting; I'll feel like a CIA mole in the KGB."

It was two weeks since Bill had heard from Nigel, when he phoned saying he was back in town and would Bill come down to the pub for a beer. Nigel was bubbling with excitement as he greeted Bill in the bar. "I heard on the news that your volcano in New Zealand has started erupting again" he chirped "and it's right on a new moon and with a perigee within twelve hours, just like you said."

"Really" Bill grinned "I haven't heard the news today."

"Yeah" Nigel replied "it was only a minor news item actually, apparently it's only a bit of a rumble at the moment. But it's amazing that it's on the new moon."

"Hmm" Bill mumbled, not wishing to sound too enthusiastic. He still felt embarrassed about his previous convictions regarding tidal forces and was now doubly wary of jumping to conclusions about the timing of specific volcanic eruptions. He changed the subject "how was your trip to the observatory?"

"Fantastic," Nigel responded "but don't change the subject, this is exciting. I have a proposition for you. Are you up for an adventure?"

"Sure what do you have in mind?"

"Well, you might have gathered that I have gotten quite rich from the oil industry. It pays quite well you know."

"Yeah I think I'm in the wrong business" Bill joked.

"My proposition is this. I'll finance us to go on a field trip to New Zealand. I propose we go over about a week before the next new moon and spend a couple of weeks over there. The next new moon's near to perigee as well. We'll do some hiking, some investigating and see if we can figure anything out. It would be an adventure."

"Like a little scientific expedition you mean?"

"Sure, but it will mainly be for fun. I hope you don't mind but I've been discussing all this with Pete and he's keen to come with us. What do you reckon?"

"Can I bring a mate of mine along too?"

"Sure, the more the merrier" Nigel agreed. "Pete's bringing a mate of his as well."

Bill was very busy with his studies but couldn't turn down this great opportunity for an adventure. He worked hard to get himself up to date before the trip.

Nigel had made all the arrangements and they met on schedule at the airport. Nigel introduced his friend Pete the astronomer who was a warm friendly man gushing with enthusiasm. "This is Fritz the loony physics teacher" he grinned introducing a short dark man with thick spectacles.

Fritz smiled "yeah don't worry about me I'm just the token nerd along for the ride."

"I feel like we're the famous five" Aaron chuckled as he introduced himself and thanked Nigel for providing this great opportunity.

On arrival in Auckland they hired a van and headed for Turangi, which was a convenient base for their expedition and just happened to be the trout fishing Mecca of the world. Bill was well aware of this and had brought his fishing gear. They had planned a couple of days of relaxation before they began their trip. Nigel was happy to busy himself making arrangements while Pete and Fritz did some sightseeing. This gave Bill and Aaron the opportunity to go fishing.

Fishing in the Tongariro River was very different to the mountain stream in Australia. The sheer volume of water was awesome, the explosive rapids and the deep pools with whirlpools and eddies made it hazardous. They had full chest waders made of rubber but they still felt the near freezing water.

"If you fall in try to let your waders fill up," Bill warned "otherwise they'll drag you under."

"Thanks for the reassurance" Aaron replied sarcastically as he cast his line into the deep water. "So you obviously brought me over here to meet these guys. Do they have potential?"

"Yes I think so, at least with Nigel. He's an old friend of mine and he's very intelligent. The other two I don't know but we should be able to assess them over the next couple of weeks. They seem pretty decent blokes and they're in fields we haven't covered yet."

"Sure" Aaron responded "and what's all this about the new moon and volcanic eruptions. Should I be worried we're going to end up like the victims of Pompeii?"

Bill laughed "I hope not. Studying eruptions was a hobby of mine when I lived in New Zealand. I think there's an increased risk of volcanic eruptions when tidal forces are at their peak. But New Zealand has a pretty good warning system and hopefully they'll tell us if they think an eruption is imminent. It's much more likely we'll die of hypothermia up there than buried in an eruption."

"Thanks, that's a comforting thought" Aaron grinned.

Bill wasn't joking about hypothermia. He had hiked around this region as a young man and knew how changeable the weather could be and the danger of being trapped on the mountain in severe conditions even during spring.

His thoughts were interrupted by a shout from Aaron who had hooked into a fish. "Bloody beauty" Bill shouted as the shining rainbow trout leapt clear of the water. The rest of the day seemed magical. They each landed several fish and kept one good one each while releasing the others. That evening they enjoyed a hearty feast, boasting to the others about the other "much bigger" fish they had released.

The next day they arose early to be greeted by a rugged looking minibus driver who was to take them to the mountain. "You guys are taking a risk, taking on Ruapehu without a guide" he said as he threw their backpacks into the vehicle.

"We'll be fine" Nigel grinned. "We've got a good map and a GPS unit." Nigel had planned the route up the mountain taking advice from a local guide. They would climb the northern side of the mountain via the Whakapapa ski field, spend two days exploring around the summit and then descend down the eastern side. They would then hike across country to climb the adjacent peaks of Ngauruhoe and Tongariro.

They were excited as they reached the Top of the Bruce where they were to take the chairlifts for the first part of the journey. The winter had provided the best snow falls for twenty years and there were still large areas of the mountain covered in snow, though the ski season was now over. The mountain was relatively quiet with only a few day-trippers and sightseers around.

The chairlift ride was serene providing magnificent views of the mountain. The trek up the mountain was quite tough going but they were in no hurry and took frequent breaks to admire the splendour of their surroundings.

Finally they arrived at their destination, the Dome Shelter and Bill gasped in awe as the Crater Lake came into view. A misty cloud seemed to clear just for them, revealing the bright turquoise lake shimmering in the sunlight. It looked almost surreal, like a fantasy picture in a fairy tale.

They made camp on a patch of gravel near the Dome Shelter while Nigel set up some portable seismic equipment he had brought with him. The new moon was due the following day.

The evening descended quickly, bringing with it the cold night air. They huddled close after eating their dinner, swapping stories of other outdoor adventures they'd been on.

It was a beautifully clear night, the stars shone brilliantly and the conversation soon turned to the cosmos. Pete was in his element, passionately describing the different kinds of stars, the blurs of distant galaxies and he explained some of the constellations. Pointing to the brightest of the Southern Cross pointers he said "That's Alpha Centauri, the nearest bright star to us, just over four light years away.

It's just mind boggling how far way it all is. Through the Hubble telescope we've seen a galaxy that's about thirteen billion light years away. If we could see just a little further we might even see the very beginnings of the universe."

"How do you figure that?" Nigel asked.

"Well of course the Big Bang theory is only a theory but it's pretty widely accepted" Pete said hesitantly. "The currently accepted theory is that the Big Bang happened about fourteen billion years ago and so if we could see that far we would be able to see it all beginning."

"Sounds a bit far fetched to me" Nigel interrupted. "I'm starting to go off accepted theories" he winked at Bill.

"Well I guess there are problems with the Big Bang theory" Pete admitted. The Big Bang conveniently explains why it all seems to be expanding that we understand from the observed redshift. But the theory assumes that the universe contains about ninety-nine percent dark matter that we can't see."

"Talk about taking it on faith, sounds like the Emperor's new clothes" Nigel quipped.

"You could be right" Pete responded. "The Big Bang theory does have quite a few flaws. The theory has a big anomaly with the mix of Helium, Deuterium and Lithium. There's also the problem of super-clusters of galaxies that would seem to have needed more time than the age of the universe to form."

"Go on admit it" Nigel chuckled "the truth is we don't have a bloody clue."

"Yeah" Pete grumbled, "OK we don't have a bloody clue."

They sat in silence for a few moments before Bill finally said "while we're talking about doubtful theories, what about the wild speculations you read in science journals these days like string theory, alternative universes and so on. We might as well just sit around smoking pot and dreaming up these theories for ourselves."

"Did you bring any?" Fritz joked.

"Sorry no" Bill smiled. "We'll have to use our God given imaginations." He gazed out into the cosmos again and said "do you reckon there are other planets out there with life like ours?"

"Has to be I reckon" Nigel replied. "Do you have anything to do with the search for extra terrestrial intelligence program Pete?"

"Not really" Pete responded "but I read about it in journals and so on. The momentum has picked up since they figured out how to predict if a star system has planets revolving around it. The closest they've found is about twenty light years away I think."

"How likely is it that we'll be able to contact them even if they are out there?" Bill asked. "How fast will we ever be likely to travel Fritz?"

Fritz responded thoughtfully "well $E=MC^2$ which means we can never get anywhere near light speed because we approach infinite mass. Let's say we'll be struggling to get even one third of light speed I reckon."

"OK, so even if we could travel one third of light speed the chances are it would take more than a human lifetime to get to any planetary system, let alone get back again. That's a bit of a problem" Bill continued. "So we might as well face the fact that we'll never be able to travel to them physically. The likelihood of an encounter of the third kind is almost zero."

Aaron who had been sitting quietly listening to the conversation at last said "I don't think we're actually meant to have contact with them. The individual souls of our human life wave are meant to find our own way. I believe the universe is built that way so we can't interfere with each other's development.

Even if in the unlikely event that some alien population with advanced technology was able to travel here they would have almost no chance of surviving our atmosphere, our diseases and so on. Their evolutionary process would have been different from ours. The science fiction writers of the twentieth century may have been entertaining but completely unrealistic."

"I agree" Bill said. "I think I'll hit the sack."

They awoke to a fine day and after a quick breakfast Nigel checked his equipment and they set off to explore the Summit Plateau region and the Cathedral Rocks. They trekked slowly and carefully over the unstable rocks and ice. The ice was extremely slippery and dangerous in places, sometimes with steep drop-offs.

Nigel was keen to lead and the others followed with Bill at the rear. He was concerned about Fritz who wasn't very fit and needed to stop quite frequently to get his breath. They reached the base of the Cathedral Rocks and had lunch before heading back to towards camp. Nigel set a cracking pace as he was concerned about the increasing cloud and Fritz started to lag behind with Bill keeping him company.

As they walked and chatted Bill completely lost track of time and hadn't noticed that they could no longer hear the talk from the other men. Suddenly he became aware that they couldn't see more than about twenty meters in front of them. "When did you last see the others?" he asked Fritz who shrugged his shoulders. Bill shouted out. There was no response. Then almost instantly the cloud enveloped them. They couldn't see a thing.

Chapter 10 - Theoretical Physics

"For the time being we have to admit that we do not possess any general theoretical basis for physics which can be regarded as its logical foundation"
Albert Einstein

Bill took out his mobile phone which thankfully had reception and called Nigel. "Bloody whiteout" he answered with concern in his voice. "Is Fritz with you, are you guys OK?"

Bill described his situation that they were OK but couldn't see more than a few feet and it had started to snow. Nigel explained that their position was slightly better. They had found a rocky outcrop under which they'd been able to take some shelter. "We'll just have to sit tight until it blows over I guess" Nigel said, "try and find a sheltered spot if you can. Trouble is I don't know how far you guys are away from us. I'm sorry I didn't notice you getting behind. You haven't got a GPS on your phone have you?"

"No we don't have that kind of fancy technology" Bill joked, "but at least we have our phones. You might want to get onto someone and see if you can find out what this weather's doing and what are our chances of getting out of here."

Bill and Fritz looked around them as best they could and found a hollow rock that was slightly more sheltered than the surrounds. They did a stock-take of their provisions which were meagre, given that they were only out for the day. Bill had most of a flask of hot coffee, a small bar of chocolate and two bananas. Fritz didn't have anything; he'd already eaten the snack food he'd brought with him. They both had quite warm woollen clothing on but Bill was concerned about them getting wet. It was starting to snow quite heavily. He had a light survival blanket and two large plastic rubbish bags. He made the rubbish bags into a makeshift raincoat for each of them. "This should keep most of the moisture off your clothes" he said. They huddled up together in the hollow and Bill shared a cup of coffee and a banana with

Fritz. "This won't stay hot all day; we might as well drink some" he said.

As they sat shivering Nigel phoned back and said "the news isn't good I'm afraid, this weather apparently came out of nowhere and they're expecting it to get worse overnight but hopefully clearing tomorrow. If we get any break in the whiteout conditions we'll try and find you."

"We'll be OK" Bill replied, trying to hide the anxiety in his voice.

For a time they kept in contact with the others by messaging on their mobile phones but then decided they had better conserve their batteries and only make contact in emergencies. The weather report was right, the wind had now come up and blizzard conditions set in.

To keep their morale up they talked. Bill had always been interested in physics and given their situation it was an opportune time to discuss it.

Fritz was obviously passionate about physics and his spirits seemed to lift as he talked. "That stuff you were saying last night about the wild speculations in theoretical physics these days" he said, "I agree with you. Theoretical physics has become more like philosophy or even a religion for some. The theories are just endless speculation with no experimental evidence to back them up. I'm almost ashamed of the lack of progress in my profession lately. We can all sit around daydreaming but what's the point?"

"I've always been fascinated by physics" Bill said "but I had trouble understanding it at school. With chemistry it was all quite clear and logical and I excelled at it, but not so with physics."

"That might not be entirely your own failing" Fritz responded. "The thing is that teachers don't really understand it either, including myself I hasten to add. As a teacher I sometimes feel inadequate to explain physics to my students. With chemistry we can explain quite well what happens at the molecular level, we can even see molecules these days. When we go to the subatomic level though, we run into problems. We don't really know what an electron is, nor a proton or neutron because we can't see them.

We only have theories about them based on their observable behaviour.

Actually I have a strong interest in nuclear physics. I'm a teacher by day but in my spare time I do some experimental work in my garage. Most people think I'm a nut case but I have a theory I've been working on that I can harness the basic energy from the nucleus of an atom in a controlled way that would provide us with very cheap energy."

"Solving our energy problem" Bill remarked. "That sounds like a noble ambition. Do you really think it's possible?"

"Sure I think it's possible, otherwise I wouldn't be doing it. Will I achieve it? I don't know. I'd like to think so. My biggest problem is funding and time. I can't get anyone to believe in what I'm doing."

"So what's the basis of your theory?" Bill asked.

"Have you heard of cold fusion?"

"Yes I've heard of it" Bill nodded.

"OK and you'll understand from Einstein's equation $E=MC^2$ that matter can be converted into energy and we use this principle to make atomic bombs."

"I guess so. Does that mean that matter is really just little bundles of energy in a different form at the lowest level?"

"Yes I believe so" Fritz agreed. "There is unlimited basic energy in the nuclei of all atoms. The conventional wisdom says that nuclear fusion reactions only take place under conditions of extreme heat and pressure. But some desktop experiments seem to show that nuclear fusion can occur at normal room temperatures and pressure resulting in excess energy. That's what I'm working on. We're only beginning to understand the relationship between matter and energy. We need to think about the nature of matter in a different way, that electrons, protons and neutrons are just little bundles of energy as you pointed out. When we use a different model it changes our perspective."

"It's a shame you couldn't pluck some of that basic energy out of the air and turn it into a nice warm heater right now" Bill shivered.

"No, but we could create a bit of heat energy by jumping on the spot" Fritz jumped up. They danced around on the spot for a few minutes which did warm them up for a time.

Bill was becoming increasingly concerned about the build up of snow around them and the howling wind. He phoned Nigel who suggested they try to build a kind of snow cave for shelter. This proved more difficult than it sounded as they didn't have any tools and shifting the snow by hand was making them wet. However they managed to make a wall that gave them some additional shelter.

"So what kind of research do you do in your garage?" Bill asked as they sat down again.

"You'll have to come and take a look at it. It's a bit hard to explain without it all in front of me. I haven't been doing the same kind of experiments as those guys with their high energy particle accelerators, but I envy their budgets. They spend billions accelerating the components of atoms and end up creating a whole range of new so-called particles that exist for a fraction of a second. Then they dream up imaginative new names for them like quarks, neutrinos and fermions and so on. But what does it mean? What have they actually achieved? How are we better off? We are really no wiser than we were at the time of Einstein's passing. We have a whole pile of theories, none proven and none with any practical application." Fritz was getting quite animated. "Sorry I'm getting on my soap box."

"No problem that's OK by me" Bill replied. "I think what you're doing is likely to achieve results because you're actually trying to solve a problem for the benefit of mankind. I think energy is the biggest problem facing our civilisation. We need people like you to be working on the problem; people who can think outside the accepted paradigm, that aren't restricted by dogma. I reckon you stand a good chance of finding the solution too because you have the desire. You have honourable intentions at heart and you're really doing it, not just talking about it."

"Thanks for the encouragement."

"No problem, do you believe in serendipity?"

"Sure I suppose so" Fritz mused. "There have been instances where scientific breakthroughs are made seemingly by happenstance. Like the discovery of penicillin, X-rays and the connection between magnetism and electricity."

"Yes but maybe it isn't just lucky chance" Bill replied. "Maybe there's more to it than that. The people who make these breakthroughs are usually actively working on solving a problem at the time. Solutions come about in unexpected and seemingly coincidental ways. But the point is we must be working towards a goal for serendipitous results to happen."

"Interesting theory" Fritz replied. "Where do you think these serendipitous revelations come from?"

"I don't know for sure. Does it really matter? I guess we can speculate. Some help may come from higher beings, from God or maybe just from the power of our subconscious minds. In any case it has to do with metaphysics."

"What do you mean by metaphysics Bill? Do you mean religion?"

"By metaphysics I mean laws of the universe that concern the nature of existence, mankind's place and so on. They include concepts like karma, the Akashic record, and spiritual planes of existence."

"Do you believe in that stuff?" Fritz enquired. "I always thought I'd like to believe in something but could never quite find anything that was logical enough. I like to keep an open mind though. So how does metaphysics work?"

"I think of it as a means of explaining our existence and our place in the universe, that there are metaphysical laws just as there are of laws of physics. For example the metaphysical law of karma states that what we do to others comes back to us."

"You mean like every action causes a reaction" Fritz queried.

"Yes something like that."

"Where do these laws exist?"

"We could say that these laws concern the etheric level and other higher planes of existence. Metaphysics also governs the hierarchy of the higher planes of existence. That is the planes that are beyond this physical world. Metaphysics explains how we can influence things with the power of our minds. This is where faith healing and other "mind over matter" things are explained."

"What's the etheric level? Is this the same ether that scientists used to imagine before quantum mechanics?"

"Perhaps," Bill replied "some imagine the ether to be like a bridge between thought and matter, or the medium in which our universe is constructed. What is the "scientific" view of the ether?"

"Well, the ether theory has gone by the wayside in physics" Fritz responded. "Scientists used to believe that the ether was the medium in which light waves travelled in. Light was considered to be a wave and, like sound waves need an atmosphere in which to travel, light waves needed the ether to travel in. Then a couple of guys called Michelson and Morley came along and did an experiment they reckoned proved the ether didn't exist. When they compared the properties of a light beam shining in the direction of the earth's spin with a beam travelling at right angles to the earth's spin, they found no difference.

Then quantum mechanics came along and the idea of light being a wave changed. The new theories didn't require an ether. But I'm not sure the Michelson-Morley experiment really disproves the existence of the ether, because we don't know the nature of the ether. Or maybe they unconsciously sabotaged their own experiment. It's interesting what you said, that physical things can be influenced by our mind. It seems that when we look at things at the quantum level that may be possible. Perhaps our thoughts do influence the results of experiments.

Michelson-Morley with that one experiment had a powerful influence on physics. The ether theory is almost universally rejected by modern scientists, despite another experimentalist by the name of Miller who later reckoned he proved the ether did exist. His experiments have been rejected by main stream physicists. But who do you believe?" Fritz scratched his chin.

"What do you think Fritz, could there be an ether?" Bill asked.

"I don't know. As I said, I like to keep an open mind. When you think about it logically there is a maximum speed limit for light in a vacuum. If there was no medium in which light travelled, you would think there would be no limit on the speed of light. Einstein said his relativity theories didn't depend on whether the ether exists or not. So we're not bound to think "ether" way. Excuse the pun" Fritz smiled.

"But why are we bound by Einstein anyway?" Bill queried. "Wasn't he struggling with his own theories late in his life?"

"Sure" Fritz stammered "his special relativity theory has been pretty spot on I think but general relativity has a lot of problems with it. And it's very complicated….."

Fritz's voice trailed off. He seemed to be drifting off. He looked very pale, and Bill gave him a shake, thinking it might not be good for him to go to sleep at this point. "Let's get up for another dance" he said. Fritz got up slowly and they jumped around madly again and cleared the snow that was encroaching into their hollow.

As they sat down again Fritz said "where did you learn about all that metaphysical stuff?"

"It's been a hobby of mine for many years" Bill replied. "I've been studying and writing about it in my spare time a bit like you working in your garage, I work in my study."

"Maybe we could get together and try to find the link between your laws of metaphysics and the laws of physics. We could come up with a grand theory of everything and blow off Stephen Hawking" Fritz chuckled.

"Why not? It has to link up somewhere. Maybe the ether is a good place to start. What do you reckon?"

"Let's see if we can't conjure up a nice hot cup of tea and a warm fire directly from the ether" Fritz laughed.

"Well I can't do that just yet" Bill grinned "but I can conjure up the last of this coffee." The last few mouthfuls of warm coffee were glorious and Bill rationed the last of the chocolate. "Look I can't conjure anything but it might be worth us saying a little prayer for some help to get off this damn mountain."

"Couldn't hurt" Fritz agreed "I'm in."

Bill said a few words of thanks to the Lord for looking after them so far and a prayer for their friends and for themselves.

“Amen” Fritz murmured, “gees its cold.” He was shivering uncontrollably.

Bill unwrapped his survival blanket and gave it to Fritz who tried to protest but Bill insisted, saying he was feeling OK. Dark set in and they huddled very close. They could no longer raise the enthusiasm for conversation. Fritz appeared to drift in and out of sleep. Bill couldn’t remember if he had fallen asleep at all. It didn’t seem as if he had when he became aware that his phone was ringing. “How are you guys faring” Nigel asked excitedly “have you noticed the weather’s clearing?”

Bill rubbed his eyes and looked around. Sure enough the sun was rising, it had stopped snowing and the clouds were starting to clear. He looked across at Fritz who was grinning back at him. “Tell him we’re alive” he said.

“Wait there” Nigel said “we’ll be with you shortly.”

Within half an hour Nigel, Aaron and Pete were standing next to them, exchanging greetings and experiences of the freezing night. It was now quite fine and they were able to make good time back to the camp. They put on dry clothes and after a hearty breakfast they all felt in high spirits. There was no question of calling off the expedition.

The remainder of the trip went without major mishap and with a good deal of enjoyment. Nigel’s equipment did not register any seismic activity, but this aspect of the trip no longer seemed important. On the last night of the hike Aaron and Bill told the others of the Science Junto project.

Chapter 11 - Archaeology

"To prejudge other men's notions before we have looked into them is not to show their darkness but to put out our own eyes." John Locke

At the next meeting of the Science Junto Nigel, Pete and Fritz were sworn in which left only two remaining vacant positions. Jeff presented his speech again to the new group and explained his covert mission. All members were called on to assist with the climate change project as the matter of highest urgency. The project was code named "Rainman" and a strategy was drawn up for its implementation. The strategy included writing letters to newspapers, to politicians and to colleagues pointing out the flaws in the climate alarmism theories and explaining the science proving that carbon dioxide emissions were not causing global warming. Each member was asked to create informal networks and to work with other groups that were working towards the same end. Jeff explained that he couldn't actively take part in this process but would continue to feed information back to the group and would give them material to use in their letter writing campaign.

Bill penned his first letter to the editor of his local newspaper as follows:

"Global temperatures are now on a cooling trend. In fact our local temperatures have been trending downwards for the last ten years. How can this be when we are spewing out more CO_2 than ever into the atmosphere? The reason is obvious. CO_2 does not cause global warming! Further proof is the fact that global temperatures went down between 1945 and 1970 whilst our CO_2 emissions were increasing dramatically.

In Al Gore's movie he makes much ado about the relationship between CO_2 and global temperatures over the long term. In this he is correct, but he has it backwards. Global temperature increase causes more atmospheric CO_2, not the other way around. This is because most of our CO_2 is dissolved in the sea. As temperatures rise, so the sea gives up more of the CO_2. There is no good science that shows CO_2 is responsible for global warming. On the other *hand there is much compelling evidence showing climate change is a natural phenomenon.*

The climate change rhetoric is being driven by environmental industries that have vested interests in the climate change scenario and it is very easy for them to sell. When someone says "you are stealing from your children" or "you are ruining the planet for future generations" this hooks people's guilt. It doesn't have to be true to be effective. Unfortunately the media has been largely responsible for the dissemination of the false information leading to the disastrous situation in which we now find ourselves.

We are about to waste billions on a carbon trading scheme that will achieve absolutely nothing except to jeopardise our economy and to succeed in lining the pockets of the confidence tricksters that have masterminded this global swindle. There are tens of thousands of scientists worldwide who have been trying to shout the truth from the rooftops yet most have received no media coverage. Many more would like to say what they think but fear for their jobs and for their sources of funding.

If our temperatures continue to trend downwards it will reduce our ability to produce food. Ironically more CO_2 *would increase our food production because* CO_2 *is plant food, not pollution."*

Bill resumed his studies with some difficulty after all the excitement of the trip to New Zealand. Nigel was still taking long service leave and would regularly meet with Bill to discuss things especially the Earth crust displacement theory with which he had become fascinated. Bill found Nigel distracting, especially when he seemed to have all the time in the world to do whatever he liked. He did enjoy the conversations however and Nigel was becoming quite active in the Science Junto.

One day Bill received an email from a young American man who was once a member of Bill's email group that read as follows:

"Hi Bill

Long time no speak! I really have missed our deep philosophical discussions on the email group. Much has happened in my life since we last corresponded. The latest is that I have secured a position in the archaeology department of your university and I'm coming to Australia to live! I'd love to catch up with you again. Maybe you could show me around?

Kind regards Jason"

Bill remembered Jason as an intelligent and thoughtful young man who was fascinated by the mythology concerning lost ancient civilisations that became very popular in the 1990s. He had taken up his studies in archaeology to pursue this passion.

He was looking forward to meeting Jason. They had corresponded on Bill's email group for several years and although they had never met in person, he felt he knew Jason quite well. They arranged to meet at the hotel where Bill had got into the habit of meeting Nigel.

Bill had no trouble recognising Jason as he walked into the bar though he looked older than the photo he remembered. He had lost his boyish looks and was tanned and rugged looking. "It's so great to meet you in person at last" he said smiling broadly as he shook Bill's hand.

"You too" Bill replied "this is Nigel."

"Pleased to meet you" Nigel responded. "I understand you're an archaeologist. That must be fascinating, what do you specialise in?"

"I used to specialise in Egyptology. That was where I was headed when I corresponded with Bill, but things have changed a bit in the last few years. Nowadays I take what I can get. I've been doing some work on the ancient Mayan civilisation lately. It might sound fascinating but the reality of it is quite mundane."

"That doesn't sound like the enthusiastic young Indiana Jones I used to know" Bill quipped.

"Yeah well the real life archaeologist is pretty much out there doing long laborious digs. Indiana Jones is pure fantasy you know."

"Are you still into all the lost civilisation stuff?" Bill asked.

"I guess so" Jason replied "but I'm afraid the old spark's not what it used to be. You might say I've been indoctrinated into the archaeological main stream. You kind of have to, to survive. I still have an open mind about ancient civilisations but at the same time I'm more sceptical, especially about all that millennium stuff that used to be around. I had the wind knocked out of my sails a few years ago too when I lost my brother."

"Oh, sorry to hear that" Bill sympathised.

"Yeah thanks. Mitch died in the nine-eleven attack. He was in one of the Twin Towers."

Jason fell silent, obviously still struggling emotionally from talking about it. He then regained his composure "I was on my honeymoon when it happened. Mitch was the best man at my wedding and then bang! A few days later he went to work at the world trade centre as usual and he never came back."

Jason hesitated again, starting to choke up. "It took me a year or so to get my head back on track, it was all very traumatic. Mitch had a wife and two young kids you know."

Bill put his hand on Jason's shoulder knowing there was nothing he could say that would help but the simple gesture seemed to calm Jason, he smiled thinly and continued. "My wife Barbara has been wonderful in helping me get through it though. We're a good team. In fact it was our common interest in ancient civilisations that brought us together. She's an anthropologist. You'll have to meet her."

"I'd love to" Bill replied. "Why don't you and Barbara come home to my place this weekend and we can catch up."

Jason nodded "thanks that sounds great, I'll talk to Barbara."

"Would you like to come too Nigel?" Bill enquired.

"I though you'd never ask" Nigel grinned. "Can I bring a lady friend?"

"Certainly" Bill agreed "is this something serious?"

Nigel blushed "she's a colleague of mine and we've been seeing quite a bit of each other lately."

Bill arranged things with Sarah who was initially reluctant to entertain so many people for the weekend. He promised he would be home early to help with preparations.

Nigel arrived first in an expensive European sports car with his girlfriend Ellen who was perhaps twenty years younger than he was. She was a cheerful bubbly girl, though Bill thought, not the intellectual equal of Nigel. He found out later that she had been his personal assistant. Bill wondered if perhaps this had broken up his marriage.

Jason arrived with Barbara soon after and they gathered around the barbeque. Barbara and Jason were obviously very much in love. She was quiet and said little, perhaps because she was shy in company.

As the evening wore on they all got on famously, which was probably helped by the consumption of several bottles of wine. Even Barbara became more talkative and the conversation turned to ancient civilisations. Ellen, who was obviously bored by such matters, went to help Sarah in the kitchen while the discussion became more intense.

"Do you still believe in the lost civilisations of Atlantis, Lemuria and so on?" Bill asked Jason.

"We're still open to it" Jason replied "but it's not the main focus of our lives any more. The archaeology profession is very much against such theories as you know and we need to earn a living."

"But we do talk about ancient mysteries in private" Barbara commented. "It's so intriguing. Not just in the old world, like Stonehenge, the Egyptian Pyramids and so on. But the Americas too, the Nazca lines, Mayan pyramids, Olmec heads, pre-Columbus artefacts in America.... so many ancient mysteries. There's just so much we don't know."

"And if we don't know it we just make it up" Jason said sarcastically.

"Now Jason, these lovely people don't want to hear about your pet hates" Barbara scolded.

"I know, sorry it just annoys me" Jason continued. "The problem with archaeology is it's so open to interpretation and the interpretation is always done to suit the agenda of the funding body or the local politics. We can dig things up, but the evidence in what we find is often so sketchy there's very little we can conclude. But we still have to come up with some story that fits the politics of the day or furthers the agenda of the financers. Sometimes I think we'd be better off writing fiction."

Nigel who had been listening intently suddenly asked "did you guys talk about the Earth crust displacement theory on your email list?"

"Sure" Jason glanced across at Bill, who nodded.

"Well it's occurred to me" Nigel continued "that if these crust displacements do occur, they must create a fair bit of volcanic upheaval, not to mention the massive rises and falls in sea levels. Sea levels were at least sixty metres lower at the end of the last ice age, or let's say when Hudson Bay was at the North Pole" Nigel winked at Bill. "Therefore if any of these civilisations existed back then, they could now be a hundred feet under the sea and we'd never know they were there. I mean look at our civilisation today. Most of it is only a few meters above sea level. If we were to be flooded like that there would be very little evidence left of our great civilisation. When were these ancient civilisations supposed to have existed?"

"Well according to Plato" Barbara responded "Atlantis went under the sea nine thousand years before his day and that would put it right around the end of the last ice age. Legends of the ancient pacific continent of Lemuria or Mu were supposed to be even earlier than Atlantis."

"So the timing could fit then?" Nigel suggested.

"Sure and then there's all the other mythology stuff" Barbara added. "Biblical floods and so on. There are folklores and stories in many cultures around the world about catastrophic floods with few survivors. The Mayans believe there have been cycles of civilisations divided by cataclysms."

"There's one big lesson in all of this for our civilisation" Bill remarked. "Even the civilisations we know about have come and gone. Civilisation isn't a one way upward progression. It comes and goes. How long have we been going? A few hundred years. Just think about what people would find about our civilisation in a few thousand years. Next to nothing. The electronic records we have these days would be useless, even the paper we use only lasts a few hundred years. The Egyptians used to write things in rock. All we'd have would be a few tombstones."

"Yeah we definitely underestimate those ancient Egyptians" Jason interrupted. He poured himself another wine, his voice was getting quite loud now as he continued "I just hate the way we patronise the ancients. These idiot theories like alien intervention annoy me most. We're told the ancients were too simple and stupid to build any of the great monuments of the past.

I blame mainstream archaeology for creating a mindset where these crazy theories can gain credence. Ancients are portrayed as dull primitive beings obsessed by superstition and weird religions. The truth is they were just like us in every way except in technology. There are just as many superstitious idiots nowadays as there were then and we know damn all more about the nature of existence than they did."

"And even their technologies can't have been too bad either to build something as amazing as the Great Pyramid" Bill commented. "Do you still follow what's going on at Giza Jason?"

"Yeah a little."

"What happened about the so-called door in the shaft from the Queens Chamber, did they ever get a robot to look through it?"

"Yes they did. They drilled a hole in the door and filmed through it but they just found another door behind it. Didn't you see Hawass on TV showing the world?"

"No, is he still in control?" Bill asked.

"More than ever. Hawass has total control of Giza these days. Everything has to go past him."

"Whoa what's all this about?" Nigel interrupted.

"It's a very long story" Bill replied. "Or should I say stories. There are many, full of intrigue and conspiracy theories abound. I'll give you some books to read. Mostly they speculate on the purpose of the Great Pyramid."

"Haven't they proved that the Great Pyramid is a tomb?" Nigel asked.

"Not at all," Jason responded "there's a lot wrong with the accepted theory that it's a tomb. The lack of decoration is a big problem. Tombs were always decorated and contained heaps of stuff the pharaoh might need in the afterlife. Yet the Great Pyramid contains nothing of that nature."

"So if it wasn't a tomb then what was it?"

"As Bill said, there are dozens of theories" Jason replied. "Many are obviously nonsense. Others are more credible, but in the end we have no idea. Again all these agendas get in the way of the truth. Now that Hawass has all the power, it's his agenda that dominates everything. That may be his Egyptian Nationalism, his ego or maybe he has some other hidden agenda, who knows? The only truth we're likely to get is what Hawass decides to reveal or not reveal to us."

"Perhaps Hawass is restricted by his superiors and by Egyptian politics" Bill suggested.

"Maybe" Jason conceded. "I guess I shouldn't jump to conclusions."

"OK, so what do we know for sure about this Pyramid?" Nigel asked.

"Well apart from the sheer size of it, the engineering is awesome" Jason explained. "The precision, the exact alignment to the cardinal points of north, south, east and west. There's a series of mysterious internal chambers and shafts that are amazing in their construction. There's a circumference relationship to height of two pi, before pi was even discovered by the Greeks."

"Yes but the Greeks made a lot of visits to Egypt" Barbara interjected. "Perhaps they got it from the Egyptians."

"Oh sure that's true" Jason continued "and maybe some information is still there. Apparently Isaac Newton studied ancient Egyptian writings."

"Perhaps in the interests of science we should go and have a look for ourselves" Nigel nudged Bill. "Who's in for a trip to Egypt?"

"Yea!" they all cheered. Jason in his exuberance spilled his wine all over the table. "Count me in" he shouted "but keep those bastards away from me."

Barbara took him by the hand and said quietly "we'd better get you to bed darling."

Once Jason was in bed Barbara returned to the table and apologised for him. She explained that the last time they were in Egypt was soon after the eleventh of September 2001 attacks and Jason had found it too confronting. "The Arabs in their Muslim dress just reminded him of the terrorists who killed his brother" she said.

"He needs to let the hatred go" Bill suggested "or it will consume him."

"I know" Barbara replied. "He is trying. He was very close to his brother you know. Perhaps he's ready for another trip to Egypt now and it might help him to let go."

The next day the idea of going to Egypt turned into a full scale plan scheduled for a month's time at the end of the current university semester. Bill had for a long time wanted to visit Egypt and the opportunity to visit the Giza pyramids with an archaeologist and a geologist was exciting. Sarah wasn't quite as enthusiastic about going all that way just to look at the pyramids, but became supportive when Bill suggested that they go on a cruise on the Nile as well.

The three couples decided to make their own individual plans and would meet up for several days to explore the Giza plateau. There was so much to organise and work to do that the month seemed to fly past and Bill and Sarah were on their way.

After a relaxing Nile cruise they arrived in Cairo and met up with the others. Nigel and Ellen had been on a brief trip through Europe and Jason and Barbara had already been in Cairo for several days. Jason had been in contact with an old colleague who was working at the Cairo museum. The colleague had recommended a guide by the name of Osama who would take them around the Giza plateau. After an evening of merriment and excited anticipation they met their guide outside the hotel in the early morning.

Osama was dressed in a typical Egyptian robe, blending in with the locals, but he spoke perfect English and was very polite. He warned them that he would need to disappear periodically for prayers as he was a devout Muslim. Jason frowned at this news but said nothing.

They took taxis to the Giza plateau and were soon queuing for entry tickets. After buying their tickets to enter the Great Pyramid, Osama advised them to wait an hour for the initial congestion of tour groups on tight schedules to subside.

While they were waiting they explored the perimeter and Bill was awestruck by the sheer size and majesty of the monuments.

Looking off into the distance he could see the head of the great Sphinx that was already starting to draw crowds.

Osama was right about the congestion which had reduced considerably as they finally went through the entrance to the Great Pyramid. He, along with all tour guides wasn't allowed to enter. After negotiating the tunnel forged by Ma'mun, the Muslim governor of Cairo who smashed his way inside in the ninth century, they found themselves at the intersection of the ascending and descending passageways.

Jason, who had been in several times before now acted as their tour guide and explained each section as they went, "past that barred gate is the descending passageway and it goes for about another three hundred and fifty feet leading to a large subterranean chamber. The subterranean chamber is quite roughly hewn and unfinished looking but interestingly the ceiling is flat and smooth."

"Is there any chance it's connected to the outside through underground tunnels?" Bill asked.

"It's possible" Jason replied "but if so the exit must be well hidden. There's been plenty of opportunity to explore it. That part of the pyramid was accessible in classical times, there's Roman graffiti down there. In those days the main entrance was being used. Apparently it was later forgotten. That's why Ma'mun had to tunnel his way in. There's a passage that leads off the subterranean chamber that goes nowhere. There's also a pit in the chamber that's filled with rubble.

The ascending passageway where we're heading into wasn't discovered until Ma'mun found it by accident as he was tunnelling his way in. See, these are the granite blocks still in place that sealed the entrance. They're impossible to remove from below, so everything you see from here on was undiscovered until Ma'mun."

They entered the narrow ascending passageway that lead steeply upwards one hundred and twenty feet into the heart of the pyramid and Bill was puffing by the time they reached the entrance to the Grand Gallery. At this point the passage branched off horizontally to the so-called Queens Chamber which was also currently barred from public access.

"Unfortunately we can't get in there" Jason muttered with annoyance "but you can see all the way down the passage to the chamber entrance."

"Isn't the passageway beautifully polished and smooth" Bill remarked, "much more so than the passage we've been in."

"Yes that is curious" Jason replied. "If they never finished the Queens Chamber you'd wonder why they would go to all the trouble of polishing the tunnel into it. The Queens Chamber itself is also finished and smoothed off except for the floor that appears to be unfinished and rough. The chamber itself is otherwise fairly uninteresting except for a niche that has no apparent function. The most intriguing features are perhaps the shafts that lead out of it. They've created so much mystery and controversy; haven't they Bill?"

"They sure have" Bill agreed. "They're so interesting because they weren't discovered until 1872 by Waynman Dixon who had to smash through the wall with a chisel to find them. So anything that's found in them must have been there since the pyramid was built."

"What prompted him to look for them?" Nigel asked.

"He apparently suspected they might exist because there are shafts in the Kings Chamber that lead to the exterior of the pyramid" Jason explained.

"Did they find anything inside these shafts?" Nigel queried.

Jason continued the story "well the problem is the shafts are only nine inches by eight inches and all Dixon could do was poke around with a long metal rod that he built up in sections. He documented finding a bronze two pronged hook, a stone and a piece of wood. The hook and the stone are still in existence at the British Museum in the original cigar box that Dixon kept them in, but the wood that we could have carbon dated is missing.

What's made all this more fascinating lately is that they've been sending robots up these shafts to take pictures. They found a so-called door at the end of one of the shafts that we were talking about. Really the door is just a slab of rock but it has some interesting copper handles on it so they've been calling it a door."

Bill interrupted "What's also interesting is that a robot took photos of what appears to be another piece of wood in one of the shafts that may have been attached to the brass hook that Dixon found. I can't understand why they don't get a robot to retrieve it. That would provide conclusive carbon dating evidence about the age of the pyramid."

Jason nodded as he motioned for them all to move forward. As they entered the Grand Gallery they saw yet another barred entrance to a shaft going downward. "That's the so-called workers shaft that goes down about a hundred and sixty feet almost vertically in places to meet the descending passageway near the bottom."

"But you said this part was inaccessible until Ma'mun" Nigel queried.

"Good point" Jason responded. "The workers shaft would have been accessible from the descending passageway, but only if you knew where the concealed entrance was. The entrance onto the descending passageway was only found in 1830 when explorers cleared the rubble in the workers shaft from the top down."

They now turned their attention to the majestic Grand Gallery. At the end of it Jason pointed upwards "see that hole up there with the cord coming out of it; that's the entrance to the relieving chambers above the Kings Chamber. That's where the famous and controversial quarry marks are, the ones that are supposed to prove that Khufu built this pyramid. Tell them about it Bill."

"OK, the controversy is about the authenticity of the so-called quarry marks" Bill explained. "There's been suspicion in some quarters that the guy who discovered them, Howard Vyse, could have forged them."

"That's right" Jason continued. "I would love to go and have a look for myself. Those marks are the only real evidence that Khufu actually built this pyramid. They're drawn with some sort of red paint. It should be possible to carbon date the paint to settle the matter once and for all. I don't know why they don't."

Jason shook his head as he led the party through the mysterious antechamber and they crawled on hands and knees into the Kings Chamber itself. As their eyes slowly became accustomed to the gloomy light they could see that it was a substantial room. At the western end of the smooth floor stood the empty granite coffer assumed by Egyptologists to be the sarcophagus that held or was to hold the body of the Pharaoh Khufu.

Their voices echoed eerily as they gathered around the sarcophagus. "What do you make of it?" Nigel asked. "It does look about the right size to hold a body. If it's not a sarcophagus for the Pharaoh's body then what's it for?"

"Well for one thing" Jason replied "there was no body ever found here and the interior of the pyramid just doesn't look like a tomb. Where are all the usual things that a Pharaoh was supposed to need in the afterlife? There's just nothing! What do you think Bill?"

"My guess is that it was for a ritual of some sort" Bill suggested.

"You mean like the sarcophagus was a kind of alter?" Barbara quizzed with an excited curiosity in her voice.

"Yes possibly" Bill continued. "When you look at the whole complex, it reminds me of a temple where rituals might take place. I've been thinking about what you said about the other chambers Jason. The Freemasons have some symbolism where a rough stone represents a rough unfinished man and the smoothed stone represents the completed man after he's been educated and built his character, his morality and so on. They also have rituals that represent the progress of the individual through various stages of personal growth. Perhaps this is a similar concept.

When you compare the three chambers, the subterranean one you said is completely rough except for a smooth ceiling. That chamber may represent the initiate before he has progressed. Then the only way up from there is through the hidden workers shaft which would have been a major ordeal. One hundred and sixty feet upwards you said, almost vertical! That would have been a major test and maybe it represents the hard road a man must travel to build his character.

Then at the next level is the Queens Chamber which is smooth except for the floor. So this could represent the man that was well advanced but not quite complete. The niche you mentioned could have been used in some kind of ritual representing that level of achievement. Then onwards and upwards through the magnificent Grand Gallery to the Kings Chamber which could be the pinnacle of achievement. The Kings Chamber then represents the completely smoothed and finished man. The granite coffer could then have been used for a final ritual for the highest level initiate. What do you reckon?"

"Hey you *have* been giving it some thought" Jason applauded. "Hell it makes more sense to me than the tomb theory. You could be onto something there Bill. The Freemasons and Rosicrucians claim to have links with this place and they both have a system of teaching and symbolism that go through various levels of attainment."

Bill nodded "yes and I think maybe symbolism is also at work here. Regardless of whether rituals actually took place here, the whole Pyramid might stand as a beacon for all mankind who are willing to see its simple message, the "meaning of life" if you like. Maybe it's the distilled essence of the great teachers and religions without the dogma; that our unperfected human souls must gradually progress through labour and virtue. The tough upward journey of the soul through the workers shaft is like choosing the narrow gate explained by Christ; the opening into the Grand Galley is like the enlightenment proclaimed by Buddhism and the coffer in the Kings Chamber represents the pinnacle of human achievement, sainthood or mastery.

"Wow, I like that idea even better" Jason exclaimed. "So *Sherlock*, maybe you could explain what these shafts are for too." Jason guided the group to one of the two shafts that led to the exterior of the pyramid. "There's been a lot of speculation lately that these have something to do with lining up with certain stars, what do you think?"

Bill scratched his chin thoughtfully "yes I've read about all that of course. They could be, but if they were meant to be sighter shafts on certain stars, why don't they aim straight out towards the sky? There's a horizontal section first, before they point upwards, so you can't take a direct line to the stars. Then I understand there are changes in direction in the shafts, they aren't actually straight. So if they have bends in them how can they be "aimed" at the stars? Isn't the conventional wisdom that they're ventilation shafts?"

"Yup" Jason nodded.

"So maybe this time conventional wisdom is right. I mean if you were going to perform rituals in here you really would need a source of air."

"OK, but what about the shafts in the Queen's Chamber?" Jason interrupted. "They don't even reach to the outside of the pyramid and they weren't open to the interior until Dixon discovered them in 1872."

"Sure" Bill replied "but maybe they were just keeping their options open. Perhaps they weren't sure if they were going to need ventilation in the Queens Chamber or not. They left only a thin section that they could easily knock out if they decided they needed the shafts. But I guess they didn't."

"You could be onto something there" Jason agreed. "So if you're right and they manage to get past the next door in the Queens Chamber shaft, they probably won't find anything except eventually the outside of the pyramid."

"I guess not" Bill shook his head.

They fell silent as several noisy tourists entered the chamber briefly and then left. For several minutes they were all silent, soaking up the splendour of the surroundings.

As Jason finally gestured for them to leave, Bill asked if he could stay on alone for a little longer. Jason smiled and nodded.

Bill remained alone in the Kings Chamber in deep contemplation for a full fifteen minutes before reluctantly retreating to join the others.

The rest of the day was spent looking around the region outside the pyramid and exploring the less interesting second and third pyramids.

After a long day, much of it in the sun, dinner back at the air-conditioned hotel was a welcome relief. They recounted the events of the day and discussed the merits of Bill's theory concerning the purpose of the Great Pyramid. Barbara, who had said little all day, finally came out of her shell and said "you might be best to keep your theory fairly quiet Bill."

"Why is that?" he responded.

"The Egyptians might see it as an attack on their culture and that their heritage is being hijacked by foreigners. To make matters worse some Muslims associate Freemasonry with Zionism."

"But that's silly" Bill replied. "There've been many Muslim Freemasons, even today."

"Yes but things have changed here in Egypt. Freemasonry has been banned here since 1964 and it's getting worse lately with the resurgence of Islamic fundamentalism. And you know the hatred that conjures."

"OK I take your point" Bill muttered. "The Freemasons are an easy target for hatred. Not just from the Muslims but also from many Christian quarters as well. They've been blamed for all sorts of things, even though their main objective is to make men into morally righteous and decent human beings from what I understand."

Nigel winked at Bill. "That just goes to show that if you're going to have a secret society it needs to be really secret" he said.

The following day the women decided to spend a relaxing day around the swimming pool at the hotel while the men explored Giza in more detail, concentrating on the area around the Sphinx. Osama had joined them again. Jason knew his way around quite well so they didn't really need Osama to guide them but they found him useful for translating and especially in discouraging the constant barrage of pushy locals trying to sell camel rides and trashy souvenirs.

"What do you reckon about the erosion on the Sphinx Nigel?" Jason asked. "There's been some speculation that the weathering is from rain and since it hasn't supposedly rained much around here since before 5000 BC it must be at least as old as that."

"Hard to say" Nigel replied. "I'd like to see some other evidence."

"I guess we'll never know for sure" Bill mused "because it's been cut out of the existing rock. But what I'm more interested in are the legends of underground tunnels and chambers around the Sphinx."

"It's more than a legend" Jason responded. "There really are underground tunnels and chambers, come and I'll show you." Jason led them back along the causeway linking the valley temple next to the Sphinx with the second pyramid. About two hundred metres along he led them down towards a subway that went under the causeway. As they approached Jason exclaimed "I'll be blowed the gate's open!" Just then there was a shout from inside and a man came out shouting "no, no, can't come here!"

"I wonder what they're up to" Jason muttered as they backed away from the entrance towards Osama who had held back and was now beckoning anxiously. They moved back to a safe distance while Jason continued to explain what was inside the subway. "Behind that gate there's a shaft with a ladder leading downwards that's also normally barred off. It was the famous shaft that Hawass exposed to the world as his fabulous discovery of the Tomb of Osiris" he continued.

"Actually he didn't discover it at all. It was uncovered by Selim Hassan in the 1930s. He explored the shaft and found chambers going off it at three levels. What Hawass did is to pump water from the bottom level. The bottom chamber is about a hundred feet down and apparently contains an empty sarcophagus."

"Another empty sarcophagus" Bill grinned. "Are their any tunnels leading off the underground chambers?"

"I believe there are but they're quite short and don't go anywhere" Jason responded.

"Are there any other tunnels around here?" Bill asked.

"You're wondering if there's a connection to the subterranean chamber in the Great Pyramid" Jason smiled. "Actually there are some underground tunnels on the Sphinx, but again they don't apparently go anywhere. Hassan found one tunnel on the rump just north of centre and another on the northern side halfway between the front and rear paws. He filled them in again after reporting finding nothing of interest. I believe Hawass may also have reopened these tunnels and sealed them over again.

There's been huge interest in the area under and around the Sphinx because of legends of a Hall of Records that were popularised by the psychic Edgar Cayce. They've had some high tech equipment around there looking for anomalies that might be chambers under the rock."

"Did they find any anomalies?" Nigel asked.

"Yes they did and they even drilled some holes back in 1978 but found nothing other than natural features. They have some better technology now but they aren't allowed to drill anymore. There's another story concerning the Egyptian Ministry of Irrigation who were drilling about fifty yards in front of the Sphinx back in 1980 and their drilling equipment hit red granite about fifty feet down. It was supposedly the same kind as in the antechamber to the Kings Chamber and there's not meant to be any natural red granite around here."

"Let's take a look over in that region" Nigel suggested.

They walked out in front of the Sphinx. There were indeed several large irrigation pumps adjacent to the seating set out for the sound and light shows but the area was otherwise fairly uninteresting. As they turned back onto the causeway Bill noticed that Jason wasn't with them and to his dismay, when he looked along the causeway he saw Jason being dragged off by a security guard.

Osama had also seen what was happening and was hurrying towards the scene. An altercation in Arabic ensued that obviously didn't go well for Osama because the guard raised his automatic weapon and Osama was forced to retreat.

"I warned him not to go into the subway" Osama complained as he returned.

"Where will they take him?" Bill asked.

"Probably just to the security office at the moment. I will need some money and maybe I can get him released."

Bill and Nigel gave all the cash they had in their wallets to Osama and followed him at a discreet distance to a security office. They waited anxiously for what seemed an eternity, but it was probably only about fifteen minutes before Osama returned followed by Jason who was grinning sheepishly.

"Sorry guys" he said "I just couldn't help myself."

"Was it worth it, did you see anything interesting?" Nigel asked excitedly.

"They grabbed me before I could get much of a look. I'll have to try and get back into the Egyptology establishment and see if I can find out what's going on there" he concluded.

Jason then went over and patted Osama on the back, praising him profusely for saving him. Osama said it was no problem he was just doing his job.

They stayed several more days in Egypt, sticking to the legitimate tourist trails and enjoying their holidays. Towards the end of the trip Barbara chose an opportune moment to thank both Nigel and Bill for bringing Jason back to Egypt. "I'm so pleased, I think he's finally moved on" she said.

Soon after returning from Egypt Bill and Sarah received a wedding invitation from Aaron and Marion along with a note to Bill suggesting another fishing trip, this time closer to home near Ebor. As they sat around the campfire Bill recounted his adventures in Egypt and his theory about the Great Pyramid. "You told me once that you knew about the significance of the Great Pyramid. Am I on the right track? Is there a link to the Freemasons, Rosicrucians and so on?"

Aaron was circumspect in his answer. "I can't tell you much more than I already have" he said. "You could be on the right track. There was a temple where Akhenaton was initiated and perhaps Moses as well. These are questions you will need to ask Hamish. As far as I know there is no direct link to the modern institutions you mention except in the way that truth and right thinking are always linked. The truth is always available to those who care to look. You've been seeking it and for the most part finding it which is a credit to you."

"Thanks" Bill replied "by the way I think I've found our last two scientists."

Conclusion

I might be wrong about many things, but then again I might be right about some of the things I have covered in this book. Sometimes the outsiders are the only ones who can see past the dogma with which the professionals have been indoctrinated during their training and in advancing their careers. Furthermore a professional is often afraid to step outside the bounds of "accepted" scientific theory, even if he has major misgivings with it.

Scientists are all human beings and are as susceptible to the same human frailties as everyone else. As a result, the scientific method in practice is not always what it is in theory. All too often the scientific establishment simply refuses to consider evidence that undermines current theories. Scientific breakthroughs are often made by a lone dissenting voice, a science sceptic or heretic.

For the sake of science and for the future of humanity we must always maintain an open mind. To progress sometimes we have to reject everything we "know" to be true, sit back and look at the evidence, see the "big picture" and apply our powers of observation, reason and experience. If you earnestly seek out the truth with an open mind, you will find it.

I challenge the readers who have got through this book to keep asking the difficult questions and continue to challenge the prevailing dogma. Don't believe everything you're told by those in authority. You are our great hope for the future. Great Truths are often very simple and stare us in the face if we will only look.

Tony Hassall